## She looked at him,
## and her heart skipped a beat.

He was smiling again, that charming, aren't-I-cute smile that skittered along her nerves. His head was tilted, and his light brown hair fell across his forehead.

"It's green."

"What?"

He nodded toward the street ahead. "The light has changed."

Lena pressed the accelerator too quickly, and the car lunged forward. She regained control and made the turn. *Watch out, Lena. Dix may seem like a nice guy, but it has only been one day. You can't afford to fall for a dimpled smile and a pair of gorgeous blue eyes.*

*Remember Peter. Remember Peter.*

## LORRAINE BEATTY

is a multi-published, bestselling author born and raised in Columbus, Ohio. She and husband Joe have two grown sons and five grandchildren. Lorraine started writing in Junior High and has written for tradebooks, newspapers, and company newsletters. She is a member of RWA, ACFW and is a charter member and past President of Magnolia State Romance Writers. Away from writing she sings in her church choir and loves to garden, spend time with her grandchildren, and travel. Visit her at LorraineBeatty.blogspot.com.

# Beautiful Dreamer

*Lorraine Beatty*

*Heartsong Presents*

To the Lord for His faithfulness. To my precious hubby, Joe, for his unfailing love and support. To my treasures, my children and grandchildren, and to the Bards. I couldn't have done this without your friendship and guidance. And especially to Joyce Hart for believing in me when no one else did.

A note from the Author:

*I love to hear from my readers! You may correspond with me by writing:*

**Lorraine Beatty**
**Author Relations**
**P.O. Box 9048**
**Buffalo, NY 14240-9048**

**ISBN-13: 978-0-373-48632-8**

**BEAUTIFUL DREAMER**

This edition issued by special arrangement with Barbour Publishing, Inc., 1810 Barbour Drive, Uhrichsville, Ohio, U.S.A.

## Chapter 1

Lena Clare Butler wanted to cry.

Spring break. She'd looked forward to this week for months and now, because she was incapable of saying no, it was all ruined. He'd be here any moment—Dixon Edwards, the movie guy. Her ball and chain for the next seven days.

It had seemed like a good idea a month ago, when her neighbor and best friend Kelly Arnez had approached her about showing a visiting filmmaker around St. Augustine. The sizable charitable donation he'd offered for the assistance had been a motivating factor as well. But now that the time was here, she was regretting her impulsiveness and cursing her deep-seated sense of responsibility that wouldn't let her back out.

She sank deeper into her sofa and looked at her to-do list for the week.

*Clean out refrigerator*
*Organize office*
*Divide and transplant cannas*
*Try out new bread recipes*
*Paint the kitchen*

Lena tossed the list onto the end table and reached for her coffee cup, swallowing the sob lodged in her throat. She would not cry about this. Crying was pointless. But her heart ached with disappointment. None of the items on her list were exciting or necessary, but she'd eagerly anticipated tackling each one.

She'd earned her masters degree earlier this year, marking the end of a long, sporadic college career. Her sisters' educations had come first. Her elementary education degree had taken nearly six years. Her masters even longer. She had taken classes in her summers off from teaching. Every holiday break, every spare minute had been spent studying and attending classes. It had all been worth the sacrifice. With degree in hand, she'd applied for the position of vice principal at her school. If she got the job, she'd be secure for the rest of her life.

Lena took another sip of her coffee. This week had been a special gift to herself. The first sweet "me time" she'd had since her parents had died and she'd become guardian for her sisters, Jeanie and Suzanna.

Now it was all gone.

The phone rang, and Lena looked at the caller ID. Kelly—the source of the upheaval in Lena's life.

"Are you ready for your adventure?" Kelly's voice was filled with excitement.

"No."

"Why not?"

"I should never have agreed to this dumb idea." She stroked her Shih Tzu, Oreo, snuggled contentedly in her lap.

"It's not a dumb idea. You're the perfect person to show Dixon around. You were a tour guide. No one knows more about St. Augustine's history than you do."

"I'm not sure I want to spend the week showing some movie director the sights."

"He's not a director. He's here scouting locations for a movie his Christian film company is making. You're not backing out on me, are you? He's counting on you."

The pleading in Kelly's voice pricked Lena's over-active responsibility gene. "No, of course not. But I had plans for the week."

"Like what? Cleaning the top of the refrigerator?"

Lena took a second to consider her friend's sarcastic question. As long as she could remember, her life had been all about survival. Making sure everything was in order. Staying on top of the financial and emotional surprises and putting her sisters first. "Time to myself for one thing."

Kelly sighed loudly into the phone. "I know, but you'll have the entire summer for that once school is out. And if you ask me, you have more than enough time alone. You need to get a life."

Lena pursed her lips. Why didn't her friend understand? "I have a life, Kelly. I have a job I love, a ministry I enjoy, and good friends. I'm perfectly content, and if it wasn't for the donation this man made to Josh's therapy pets program, I would never have agreed at all."

Her friend, veterinarian Josh McDowell, started a ministry to bring animals to visit patients in nursing homes and rehabilitation centers. She and Oreo were regular participants, but a sluggish economy had caused a substantial drop in donations. The program was in danger of closing.

Edwards's contribution would ensure the ministry's survival awhile longer.

"You could have said no."

Lena gripped the phone. "And see the pet therapy program close? I couldn't let that happen."

"Then helping Dixon is a fair trade, right?"

Her friend had a valid point, but while she appreciated his donation, it didn't lessen her uneasy feeling about him. "Are you sure this guy is legitimate? Anyone can claim to have a Christian ministry."

"Of course he's legit. I told you, Dixon and Rick went to college together. That's the reason he's staying with us and not at a hotel. What's this about, Lena? It's not like you to be so suspicious of people."

Lena absently combed her fingers through Oreo's coat. "I'm merely being cautious."

She'd sized Edwards up at church yesterday when he'd addressed the congregation. Had she met him beforehand, she would never have agreed to help him. Ever. Dixon Edwards was charming, friendly, and magnetic, with a smile that could convince people to part with their money and their common sense for any so-called worthy cause.

The way her ex-fiancé, Peter Cane, had bilked the small church in Tampa out of thousands with his phony mission scam. He'd stolen the money and stolen her heart and left them both shattered.

Lena jumped at the loud knock on her front door. "He's here."

"Oh. Yeah, that's why I was calling. To tell you he was on his way over."

"Thanks for the warning." She hung up the phone, her heart pounding. As much as she dreaded spending this week with Edwards, she was looking forward to revisiting all the sights of St. Augustine. Though she doubted a self-absorbed man like Edwards would appreciate her lovely hometown.

Her conscience stung, and she offered up a quick prayer for forgiveness. She shouldn't be pigeonholing Dixon Edwards before she actually met him. Her mistake with Peter was a long time ago, and God had healed her broken heart. But He'd also shown her a major flaw in her own character—a tendency to fall in love quickly with charming men. Like Edwards.

Her guard would be up.

The knock came again. Lena inhaled a fortifying breath, forced a smile, and opened the door. Oreo barked excitedly at her feet.

"Miss Butler, I'm Dixon Edwards." He glanced down at Oreo, who was sniffing at his boots.

Lena stared at the man on her doorstep. He looked different than she'd remembered him from yesterday. He seemed taller, leaner, and more imposing. The broad shoulders inside his burgundy button-up shirt tapered to narrow hips and long, jean-clad legs.

She hadn't noticed how his light brown hair fell roguishly across his broad forehead and softened his generous mouth and full lips.

He was more vital up close. The masculine energy emanating from him was disconcerting. She swallowed and struggled to find her voice. "Nice to meet you, Mr. Edwards." He smiled and grasped her hand. The contact sent a shiver up her spine and made her knees wobble strangely. She tugged loose and adjusted her glasses. She'd been right to keep her guard up. Edwards was already doing strange things to her nerves.

"I appreciate you helping me out this week." He stepped inside, placing a large case and notebook at his feet. He closed the front door behind him. "It'll go a lot faster with a local showing me around."

He smiled again, and Lena found herself searching for something to say. The dimple in his left cheek softened the angled planes of his face and brought a twinkle to his sky blue eyes. She forced herself to concentrate on the task at hand. "So what exactly will we be doing? Kelly said you needed help finding places in St. Augustine for a movie?"

"Right. I'm here scouting locations to use in a film we'll be shooting here next year. My location manager normally does this job, but she's out on maternity leave. Since there wasn't a local professional to work with, the job fell to you."

Lena frowned, still unclear of his purpose. "So you're here sightseeing?"

Edwards smiled and crossed his arms over his chest. "In a manner of speaking. I'm doing an overall look-see this trip. Tina, the location manager, will come back in a few months with the production team and do a more detailed scout." Oreo rose up and put his paws on Edwards's legs. "Is this your charity?" Edwards reached down and scratched the black-and-white dog's head. "Kelly said something about animal hospitals."

"No. Animals *in* hospitals."

Edwards frowned. "Isn't that unsanitary?"

"Therapy pets," Lena explained. "We bring animals to visit patients in hospitals, rest homes, and rehabilitation centers. Stroking pets is calming and reassuring when people are hurting." A sweet memory came to mind. "There was an elderly lady in the home we first visited. Mrs. Carter. She was so cranky, so sad, but when she held Oreo, all that faded away. She changed in front of my eyes. It was so rewarding."

He grunted under his breath. "Interesting."

Lena was more interested in her role in this agreement. "And what do we do when we find some of these locations?" Edwards smiled again. She wished he'd stop doing that. She couldn't think clearly. That dimple made him look like a mischievous little boy.

He spread his hands wide. "Lots of things. First I'll take pictures for overall aesthetic of the city. A few stills. A little video and some panoramic. Then we'll hunt down specific sites to match the script. I'll look into the logistics and feasibility of each site—how far is it from the base of operations, is parking available, is the nearby electrical power sufficient, or will we need generators? Light sources and sound levels for each site need to be checked. Weather conditions have to be assessed. Then I'll have to obtain permission and cooperation from location owners of the sites and their neighbors. Also local governments and law enforcement."

Lena tried to digest all he'd told her. "I had no idea there was so much involved."

"Most people don't."

Edwards rested his hands on his hips, and she couldn't help but notice the strong forearms below the rolled-up sleeves of his shirt. His hands were broad with beautifully tapered fingers. She forced herself to concentrate. "So you really do own a movie company?"

He grinned. "Yes, I really do. Co-own, actually. Larry Austin is the majority partner."

Lena knew better than to take anyone at face value. "So would I know any of your movies?"

Edwards shook his head. "Probably not. Up until recently, we've only made small promotional films and corporate videos. We branched out a few years ago into feature films. The first one will be released this summer.

The one we're shooting here in St. Augustine is our second big-budget production."

Lena's guard rose a notch. Talk was cheap, and something about Dixon Edwards made her uneasy. "So could I see some of your work?" She gauged him closely, preparing to analyze his response.

"Sure, but I doubt you'd find them interesting. I can get you a copy of the upcoming release if you'd like."

She started to say yes, just to see if he could actually produce it, but then she reminded herself to dial down the doubt. Edwards was a good friend of Rick and Kelly's. She had no reason to question anything he said—except her own gullible history. "No thank you. I doubt if I'd have time to watch it."

He held her gaze a moment, and she realized he was waiting for her to make the next move. "Oh. I'm ready if you are." She grabbed her purse from the foyer table then opened the door. The sooner they got started, the sooner she'd be done with the man.

"Right." He picked up his gear and followed her outside to the car.

They climbed in, and Lena started the engine. "Where do you want to go first?"

Edwards shrugged then adjusted his seat backward several notches to better accommodate his large frame. "Wherever you like." He smiled, holding up a thick notebook. "I have a lot of ground to cover."

Lena was more certain than ever that she'd made a huge mistake in agreeing to show this guy around. His quick smile and even quicker tongue meant she'd have to be vigilant. God had revealed her vulnerabilities, but it was up to her to maintain control of her life.

"Surely you have a starting point?" She put the car in

reverse then looked at her passenger. His expression was pleasant but unreadable.

"Not really. Pick a direction and go for it."

Lena frowned. "Which direction?"

Edwards chuckled. "You don't like being spontaneous, do you?"

"Mr. Edwards—"

"Dix."

She sighed audibly, hoping he'd get the hint. She was running out of patience. "Dix, I'm here to assist you, but I can't do that if you won't tell me where you want to go and what you want to see. We have to have a plan. We can't simply drive willy-nilly all over town."

Edwards stared at her, his blue eyes probing and intense. She looked away, uncomfortable with the scrutiny. "Do you want the beaches? The Castillo and all the other tourist traps? Or are you looking for a church, a house, a business?"

He smiled, his grin impish. "Yes."

Lena grunted, which only made him chuckle more. She'd given up her spring break for this guy?

"Sorry. I'm teasing you. You remind me of my sister. She couldn't make a decision either unless there was a road map laid out."

Lena bristled. "I am perfectly capable of making a decision, and your sister sounds like a very sensible woman."

"That she is."

He glanced out the window. She turned the car around and pulled to a stop at the end of her driveway. She drummed her fingers on the steering wheel while he made up his mind.

"Why don't you start with the usual tourist stuff? I'll let you know if I see something I think will work for specific scenes."

Lena pulled out onto Inlet Drive, heading toward the west side of Anastasia Island and the Bridge of Lions that joined it to historic St. Augustine. She tried to ignore the man beside her, but his energy seemed to suck the air out of the vehicle.

The silence between them grew uncomfortable as they waited for the light to change, but Lena was reluctant to start a conversation. She'd agreed to play tour guide. Bonding with the man was not on her agenda. Keeping a safe distance was.

"This bridge is amazing." Dix glanced at her briefly then turned back to the passenger-side window. "I crossed it on my way to Rick and Kelly's the night I arrived. Impressive."

Lena allowed herself a moment to appreciate the unique beauty of the recently restored landmark. She never tired of driving over the bridge to work every day, being suspended between the Matanzas River below and crystal blue sky above. There was something magical about passing between the four gothic towers at the center of the span and seeing the colorful buildings and red-tiled roofs of the city in the distance. "Yes it is. It was completely renovated a few years ago."

"How old is this bridge?"

She glanced out at the sailboats on the water and sun glinting off the whitecaps. "The bridge was built in 1927. It's a double-leaf bascule drawbridge, and it's listed on the National Register of Historic Places. The marble lions on the west bank were donated by a friend of Henry Flagler's."

"Wow. You really know your facts."

"I used to work as a tour guide."

"Now I know you're the right one for the job. Flagler. The guy responsible for making Florida a tourist mecca?"

"That's right." Lena merged to the right, driving past

the Queen palms that marked the end of the bridge. March was a great time to explore St. Augustine. The weather was warm but not hot, the breeze gentle and fragrant, and hurricane season was months away. She'd concentrate on that and not on the man she was with. It would be easier that way.

"So, how long have you been making movies?" The silence was getting to her. So was his frequent scrutiny.

"For about eight years now. Ever since I left my day job."

"What was that?"

"I owned a marketing company."

Lena glanced over at him. Was he serious? "You left a perfectly good job to play around with movies?"

Dix arched an eyebrow. "Play? Making movies is hard work. Making Christian movies is even more work. I have to make sure the message is square with the Word."

The twinkle in his eye made her uneasy.

Dix leaned forward and peered over at her. "You don't approve, Ms. Butler?"

Lena kept her gaze on the road ahead. "My name is Lena, and it's none of my business."

"But you think it's irresponsible, don't you, Lena?"

Hearing him say her name created an odd fluttering sensation in the center of her chest. "You don't walk away from a job with a solid future for something that's iffy."

"Sure you do. People do it all the time. It's called following your dreams."

"It's foolish."

Dix nodded thoughtfully. "And you never do anything foolish?"

"Not on purpose."

"Or impulsive?"

"No. That only leads to disaster."

Dixon chuckled softly. "That depends on how you define disaster."

Lena turned the car north onto Avenida Menendez toward the Castillo. What did he mean by that? A disaster by its definition was bad. And at the moment, disaster was the perfect word for the mess she was in.

Showing this man around for a week was a disaster waiting to happen. Maybe it wasn't too late to get out of it. Edwards's donation had been a huge blessing to Josh's program, but maybe she could help Josh financially later, after she got her promotion. She glanced over at her passenger. At Dix. He grinned and winked, and her heart sank.

Oh yeah. Great big disaster.

Dixon Edwards stole a glance at Lena as she drove. She hadn't spoken since his comment about disaster, and her disapproval was evident. Her chin was tilted upward, her lips pressed firmly together, and her shoulders squared with the steering wheel. He glanced at her hands and wanted to laugh out loud. Yep. As he suspected. Placed at the recommended two and four o'clock positions. Lena was a by-the-book kind of lady.

He swallowed the chuckle that rose in his throat. Miss Lena Butler was one set-in-her-ways woman. He liked her though. She was exactly like his sister Denise had been before he straightened her out. All rules and plans and following directions. Committed to always doing the right thing and afraid of taking a chance on anything.

But he had to admit she was pretty cute behind the glasses that did nothing to hide her lovely green eyes. Her thick coffee-brown hair fell straight to her shoulders then curved slightly at the ends. He was curious about her smile. So far all he'd seen was a frown of disapproval and a wide-eyed look of surprise.

She wasn't exactly what he'd expected. Kelly had described her friend as sweet and kindhearted, a dedicated teacher vastly knowledgeable about her hometown. Kelly had failed to mention she was also an uptight control freak. Maybe he could work on her the way he had his sister. It might be fun to teach his guide to relax and learn to be spontaneous.

He stole a glance at Lena again. His sister's need for control stemmed from a childhood accident. What was Lena's story? The memory of her sweet expression when she'd talked about the woman at the home came to mind. Her affection for the elderly was obvious. Behind Lena's control-freak exterior was a woman with love and compassion. He wanted to learn more about that Lena.

The car slowed, pulling into a long, narrow parking lot. "We'll start at the Castillo de San Marcos." Lena turned off the engine. "It's one of our most treasured landmarks and dates back to the late sixteen hundreds."

Dixon looked up and saw the thick stone walls of an ancient fortress perched on the edge of the bay. Dark gray and massive, it stood in stark contrast to the delicate palms that dotted the perimeter.

Dix got out of the car, scanning the area. "Wow. I saw this place Saturday night when I drove in. Good job." Retrieving his equipment from the backseat, he pulled his camcorder and headphones from the case and hung them around his neck. He hooked the light meter onto his belt. Lena joined him as he surveyed the area more closely.

"What do we do now?"

"We take pictures." He transferred a stack of papers from his notebook to his clipboard.

"Of what?"

"Everything." He started toward the sidewalk leading to the Castillo. "This place is amazing."

Lena walked at his side. "The fort has never been captured and stood under three different flags. Spanish, British, and American."

Dix stopped and took a few panoramic pictures of the fort, listening as Lena explained about the four bastions and their unusual positioning to create a crossfire should intruders approach.

Through his lens the Castillo resembled a dark jewel mounted in a setting of vibrant green grass. He allowed himself a moment to appreciate the view. "This fort is right out of a pirate movie. I can imagine the ships out there in the bay, cannon fire lighting up the sky. I could do an entire film on this site alone."

"I know." Lena smiled at him over her shoulder, brushing her hair from her face. "I never get tired of seeing it."

Dix found himself unable to look away. He'd wondered what her smile would look like, and now he knew. Beautiful and dreamy.

But something behind her smile and reflected in her green eyes was in opposition to the controlled woman he'd seen so far. There was a longing in her eyes. But a longing for what? As he watched, her gaze turned wary, and she crossed her arms over her chest. What was she so afraid of? Him? Or something else?

"We could take in one of the cannon firings if you'd like. They do them several times during the day."

"Good idea." Dix forced himself to concentrate on his work and not the growing questions about his guide. Walking out onto the broad expanse of lawn, he tried another photo angle of the Castillo. He glanced down at the ground, fascinated by the vine-like grass. Its runners shot out in odd angles across the sandy soil, piling upon itself until it made a thick, spongy, green carpet. It bore little resemblance to the carpet of bluegrass back home in Nashville.

Everything here was different from home, and the balmy weather was only the most obvious. He'd been to the Atlantic Coast several times and Miami several years ago, but there was something different about St. Augustine. He inhaled a deep breath of warm, salty air. There was a friendly feeling about the place and a relaxed, easygoing pace of life. Maybe it was the soothing blues of sky and water contrasted with the vibrant green foliage. Or maybe the charming pastel buildings and red-tiled roofs, or the white crystal beaches and the sailboats in the bay.

Whatever it was, he liked it, and he'd be sorry to leave it behind at the end of his stay.

He glanced back at Lena, who was waiting patiently for him on the sidewalk. He had a feeling he might miss his tour guide when he left, too. He was looking forward to getting to know her better. An idea came to him. He returned to the sidewalk and smiled at Lena. "Help me out, will you?"

She looked skeptical. "Doing what?"

Dix hid his grin. She was more like his sister than he'd thought. It would be fun to push a few of her buttons and see if he could teach her to roll with the punches a bit more. He picked up his clipboard and handed it to her. "Keep track of the sites as I shoot them, and tell me what I need to look for next."

"Oh." Lena took the clipboard reluctantly, her green eyes wide with surprise. "I don't know anything about this job."

He smiled at her confused expression. "You probably know as much as I do. I'm filling in for the regular scout, remember? See these sheets?" He pointed to the one on top. "Each page is a scene in the movie I need to locate a site for. The sections to the right are for logistical data. Things like availability of electric, water, accessibility for crew and equipment." He stopped and peered at Lena. She looked dazed.

He decided to push his by-the-book guide a bit more. "The box to the left is for listing names and phone numbers of people or organizations that I'll need to obtain permission or permits to do the actual filming. Do you know anyone with the Chamber of Commerce?"

Lena blinked and shook her head. "No. I don't."

"Too bad. Do you need a pen?" Lena looked as if she might go into shock.

"I'd like some time to look this over." She sifted slowly through the worksheets. "I want to understand what I'm supposed to do."

"No time." Dixon took her arm, steering her toward the fortress and stifling the smile that teased his lips. She definitely liked being in the driver's seat. "You'll get the hang of it soon enough. Just write down what I tell you, and let me know what the next scene is. Do you know how to use a digital camera?"

They started toward the entrance to the massive fortress, and he stole one more glance at his companion. She was scurrying to comply with his request.

Oh yes, it was going to be an interesting week.

# Chapter 2

The Coquina Café was tucked away on the corner of two historic St. Augustine streets a block from the Castillo. The patio area was sheltered by Spanish moss-draped live oaks and colorful umbrellas, offering a soothing respite from the sun and the activity of the morning.

Lena took a bite of her sandwich, sighing with pleasure at the taste. Normally she didn't eat a big lunch. Not much time for that when she was teaching. Today, however, she was exhausted and needed to restore her energy and her spirits.

While touring the perimeter of the Castillo earlier, Dix had spotted a potential location. They'd crossed the street to take pictures, but then he'd become distracted by another possibility on Charlotte Street, which had ultimately led to the little café. She'd convinced him to take a lunch break before they continued on. They'd chosen a table in a quiet corner, for which she was grateful. She needed time to catch her breath. And fill her stomach.

Working with Dixon Edwards was like living inside a washing machine. He changed his mind, changed directions, and changed plans faster than she could keep up. They'd spent most of the morning touring the Castillo. Dix had taken countless pictures and video of the historic structure and made endless notations. He'd also spoken at length with the national park ranger on duty. She'd pointed out every detail and historic tidbit she had at her disposal. Assuming her old tour guide role had helped her keep a safe, impersonal distance to Dix's overwhelming enthusiasm.

She'd tried to make some sense out of his worksheets, but her lack of knowledge about the job made it difficult. The pages weren't in any particular order. Page one was scene twenty-eight. Page two, scene 5. Each scene requirement was very specific. Stone wall with window. Sidewalk outside homeless shelter. Corner store with mailbox.

But Dix would walk past a potential location for one scene in search of a site in another. His search pattern was totally illogical, but when she pointed out the inefficiency of his methods, he assured her it would all get done and not to worry. Dixon's haphazard approach to his job had given her a headache.

She glanced over at him standing off near the restrooms, talking on his cell. She wasn't sure what to make of Dixon Edwards. She could never be sure when he was being serious and when he was teasing. She wondered sometimes if he was really scouting locations or merely taking her on a wild goose chase.

No. Whatever she thought of his methods, she couldn't doubt his dedication to his work. She took another bite of her sandwich while Dix ended his call. Maybe she could convince him to let her arrange the search order for tomorrow. They'd accomplish more and finish sooner. Which might salvage some of her precious "me time."

Dixon returned to the table and took a sip of his drink. "Sorry about that. Business. Looks like I'm going to China."

Lena wasn't sure she'd heard him correctly. "You're going to China?"

"Beijing. One of the perks of my job. My partner doesn't like to travel. He's married with kids, so I get to do all the leg work."

Lena tried not to stare. She'd always dreamed of traveling to foreign lands. China was at the top of her list. But that wasn't possible until her future was secured.

"So, I never asked you. What's this movie about?" She had to admit helping Dix today had made her curious about the filmmaking process. She wasn't so curious about Dixon Edwards. The less she knew about him, the better.

"A minister who leaves the pulpit and the little girl who helps him return."

"It sounds like a good story."

Dix nodded in agreement. "I've got a copy of the script if you'd like to read it. Kelly's about finished with it, I think."

"No, thanks." She had little interest in the story. What she really wanted to know about was the places he'd traveled. But she didn't want to seem too inquisitive.

Dix took a healthy bite of his sandwich. "Kelly tells me you teach little kids."

"First grade." She wondered how she'd become the topic of conversation. She'd about given up on trying to discern Dix's train of thought. "But I'm hoping to move into administration soon."

"Oh. Why's that? Kids wearing you down?"

"No, certainly not. I love teaching, but the vice principal's position would mean a more secure future."

"Why's that?"

Lena frowned. "Because a job in administration is very stable. Security is important."

Dix raised an eyebrow. "To whom?"

Was he mocking her? "Everyone."

He studied her intently for a moment then stood. "Pictures."

"What?" Why did the man have to be so unpredictable? She'd quit right now if she could, but she'd made a commitment, and she would abide by it. God expected her to be responsible. "Pictures of what?"

"Here. The courtyard." He glanced around. "It's perfect for scene fifteen." When the waiter approached to pick up the check, Dix caught his attention. "Is the owner here today? Could I speak with him please?"

Lena watched as Dix proceeded to gain permission to photograph the restaurant, exchange information, and explain what would happen if the business was chosen for the shoot. It really was impressive to watch Dix work. He'd been warm, friendly, and sincere as he'd talked to the owner.

Lena joined him near the stone wall surrounding the patio as he pulled out his camera and began taking pictures. "He'll be disappointed if you don't use his restaurant in your movie."

"I wouldn't have told him that if I wasn't reasonably sure. That would be wrong."

Lena felt chastised. At least Dix possessed a measure of ethical awareness. "Where to next?"

He smiled and winked. "What's next on our list?"

She ignored the heat his flirtation sent into her cheeks

and flipped through the worksheets on the clipboard, attempting to match scene requirements with places she knew.

Dix abruptly took her arm and turned her toward the street. "Let's walk. I want to see more of your city."

Lena held up the clipboard. "But there are places on here we need to find."

Dix shrugged as they strolled out onto the sidewalk. "But it's a beautiful day." He inhaled deeply and looked at the sky. "I could get used to all this sunshine and water. This is a charming city."

"Yes it is."

"It reminds me a lot of New Orleans with the quaint buildings, the wrought iron, and narrow streets."

Lena flipped over a sheet on the clipboard. "There's a small copse of trees in scene thirty. I think I know a place near Flagler College that might work."

"Did you hear what I said?"

"Yes. It's a charming city. I know. I look at it every day."

"Ah, but do you really see it?"

"Yes. And it resembles New Orleans because they both have Spanish roots." She glanced at him, and her heart skipped a beat at the look in his blue eyes. Part teasing, part appreciative, part probing. What was he searching for? To see how gullible she might be? How susceptible to his charm?

She turned away, ashamed of herself. She had to stop trying to cast Dix in the same mold as Peter. She was being judgmental and unfair. Totally against her character. Unfortunately, being attracted to charming men like Dixon wasn't.

"We'd better get back to work." She used her stern teacher voice, hoping to get his attention. At the rate they were going, Dixon Edwards would have to take up residence to get all his locations scouted.

Why did that sound like a good idea?

Twilight waned while Lena curled up with her book in the lounge chair on her lanai. After a shower and a light supper, the tension of the day was finally easing.

Dixon had returned to Kelly's, and she was looking forward to a long, quiet evening alone. She needed as much downtime as possible before working with him again tomorrow.

The evening air was thick with the heady fragrance of jasmine and orange blossoms, with a tinge of chlorine from the pool. The comforting aromas of life in a beach town. She leaned back and closed her eyes, allowing the soft rustle of the palm fronds in the breeze to relax her even more. Until the soothing evening sounds changed to approaching footsteps.

"So? How did it go?"

Lena laid down her book and glanced at Kelly as she entered the lanai and hurried across the patio. "How did what go?" She really didn't want to discuss her day with Dix.

"Don't be obtuse. You know what I mean." Kelly sat down at the foot of the lounger. Oreo jumped up and joined them.

Lena exhaled and shook her head. "I don't think I'm the right person for this job."

Kelly touched her arm lightly. "Why? Did something happen? I mean, Dix seems like such a nice guy. Friendly and charming."

Lena nodded and crossed her arms over her chest. "Oh he's charming all right, and he knows it. But he's completely disorganized and irresponsible."

"And that's a bad thing?"

She glared at her friend. "Kelly. You're an accountant. You understand the need for order and structure. This man goes off in a different direction every time he has a new thought."

"Well, he is the creative type, you know. They see the world differently than we ordinary people do."

"Creative? More like chaotic."

"Oh, I don't know," Kelly said with an impish smile. "I think he might be good for you. You could use a little loosening up. Get away from your calendars and lists."

Dix had said the same thing earlier, but they were both wrong. "There's nothing wrong with being organized."

"There is when it rules your life and you can't make a move without it."

Lena exhaled in disgust. "Didn't I change my plans for this week and agree to work with him?"

Kelly nodded, grinning. "Yes, and I appreciate it. But I know you're reworking your to-do list every second, trying to keep your life under control."

Lena glanced down at the notepad slid between the pages of her book. Her friend wasn't wrong, but did she have to make it sound like a bad thing? "If I don't keep track of my obligations, something is liable to fall through the cracks."

"And? So what if it does?"

Didn't anyone understand? "I can't simply ignore my responsibilities."

Kelly frowned. "I'm not talking about not paying bills or missing doctors' appointments. I'm talking about re-scheduling time to clean the closet, transplant flowers, or even rent a movie. You're a slave to schedules, Lena."

"You're exaggerating. I like to keep track of things that need to be done, that's all. Unlike your friend. He had a list of places to look for but he never looked at it."

Kelly laughed. "Oh, I get it now. Dixon made you crazy because he was spontaneous and impulsive and that grated on every nerve in your body, didn't it?"

Lena rose and placed her book on the patio table. "No. But he was so cavalier about everything. He'll never get all his locations selected if he goes about it like he did today."

Kelly shrugged. "Maybe you should go with the flow and be spontaneous like he is. Or don't you think you can?"

Lena planted her hands on her hips. "Of course I can. I can be as spontaneous as the next person."

"Yeah, right." Kelly stood, a skeptical grimace on her face. "I called you last week on the spur of the moment to go antiquing, and you turned me down. Why?"

"Because I had grocery shopping to do."

Kelly laughed out loud. "I rest my case." She started back across the patio.

Lena felt a need to defend her decision. "There wasn't anything in the house to eat."

"The stores are open 24-7."

"If I hadn't gone, then I would've had to rearrange everything." She followed her to the screen door.

Kelly chuckled. "You're rigid."

"I am not."

"Hello, ladies."

Dixon Edwards stood on the other side of the lanai door. Smiling. Lena's heart skipped a beat. Even in the twilight, his smile was dazzling. Not that it mattered.

"Hey, Dixon. Did you have a productive day?" Kelly asked, patting his shoulder as he stepped into the lanai.

"Very. Thanks to Lena." He smiled at her, his blue eyes holding her gaze.

If he'd announced he was running for dogcatcher she wouldn't have been more surprised. They'd only found a fraction of the sites on his worksheets.

"That's our Lena. Productivity is her middle name."

Lena glared.

"That's good to know, because I need your services again." He smiled sheepishly and rested his splayed fingers on his hips.

"Do you want to start earlier tomorrow?" Lena tried to calm her racing pulse and mentally reworked her list. She could move cleaning the bathroom back to tomorrow night, and the laundry could be done this evening between bathing Oreo and finishing her book.

Dix rubbed his forehead. "Well, actually I'd like you to come with me this evening. I want to take some shots of the Castillo at night. I think it might make good stock footage."

Lena stared at the man in front of her. Was he serious? He certainly looked like it, but who could tell with him? "You mean right now?"

"Sure. Why not?"

"Yeah, why not?" Kelly echoed with a smirk.

"Because I have things to do. And it's late."

"It's not that late, and I'm sure whatever you were going to do can wait." Kelly's voice dripped with sarcasm.

"No, that's all right." Dixon held up his hands. "I did spring this one on you, Lena. I'll understand if you can't help me out."

Lena's sense of responsibility stirred. She had promised to be his guide for the entire week. She hadn't laid out any rules or boundaries, something she saw now was clearly needed. Kelly had challenged her about being spontaneous. But she did have things to do. Not life-altering, granted, but basic, everyday responsibilities that had to be addressed.

But going out with Dix at night didn't appeal to her at all. "Perhaps you could go alone this time. The fort's not hard to find."

Dixon shook his head. "I'm afraid I wasn't paying any

attention to how we got there today. I was focused on the imagery, not the directions."

Lena's resolve was starting to shift under her feet like sand on the beach. She resisted. The last thing she wanted to do was spend more time with the overly charming and attractive Dixon Edwards. "Maybe we could schedule it for tomorrow night."

"It's supposed to rain tomorrow night. I have to make the most of every moment." He pinned her with his blue gaze. "And I'll only have your expert company for this one week."

The dimple in his left cheek flashed, and her resistance crumbled. She had made a commitment, after all, and she was obligated to honor it. Even if that meant tossing her own plans into the air. Her stomach knotted at the thought of shifting mental gears so suddenly. "Well, I suppose I could. But I'll need a few minutes to get ready."

"You kids have fun." Kelly winked and waved goodbye. "Oh Dixon, do you have your house key?"

"Yes, but I'm coming back to get my gear." He turned to Lena. "Let's meet at your car in ten minutes."

She nodded, wondering when she'd forgotten how to say no. She turned and walked into the house, Oreo on her heels. Instead of a nice quiet evening reading and doing a few chores, she was traipsing downtown again with a man who thought spur of the moment was the only way to live.

Lena ran a brush through her hair and quickly changed into a pair of slacks and a matching top and jacket. The breeze off the water from the Atlantic, even in the sheltered inlet, could be cool this time of year. It could also be incredibly beautiful and romantic. Something she did not want to experience with a man like Dixon. A man who reminded her too much of Peter.

She'd been shamefully susceptible to Peter Cane. He'd

smiled, said a few pretty words, and she'd followed him like a puppy, right into humiliation and heartbreak. How could she have been so gullible? She'd believed everything he said. She'd believed in his ministry to help bring medical care to children in the Appalachians.

But it had all been a lie. Fool me once. She'd have to be on guard against Dixon's knockout smile and his unusual ministry. She couldn't afford to make that mistake again.

"I really appreciate this, Lena." Dixon settled into the passenger seat and fastened the safety belt.

"I don't go out much at night unless it's a school or church function." She wasn't sure why she'd said that.

"I can understand that. My sisters are the same way, and I can't say I blame them. A woman on her own has to be careful."

"How many sisters do you have?" She regretted the question immediately. The less she knew about Dixon, the better.

"Three. Denise, Vicky, and Frankie. I'm the baby."

"That explains a lot." Obviously the man was used to being the center of attention.

"I don't think I'll ask you to clarify that remark. What about you?"

"Two. Jeanie and Suzanna."

"Interesting names."

"We were born upstate in White Springs, a town famous for the Stephen Foster State Park."

Dix smiled. "I get it. 'Oh Suzanna.' 'Jeanie With the Light Brown Hair.' What's the song you're named for?"

"A very obscure one called 'Gentle Lena Clare.'"

"Good choice."

She glanced at him, but he'd already turned to look out the passenger window.

"What's that island out there?"

"That's part of Anastasia State Park," she said, pulling out onto Inlet Drive.

"You have a prime location with your house. On the water, your own pier. Nice."

"My dad inherited it from his parents. We moved here when my sisters and I were small."

"Ever think about selling, moving someplace else?"

Lena frowned. "This is my home. I was raised here."

"I know, but don't you ever get the itch to live someplace new, see something different when you wake up each morning? Not that the ocean view isn't spectacular."

"My home is paid for. It's my investment for my retirement. Why would I leave?"

Dixon turned and smiled at her, his eyes bright with excitement. "Adventure. You can't tell me you don't long for adventure, Lena Clare."

Her cheeks grew hot, and her heart pounded. How did he know? What had she said or done to reveal her secret? "No. I don't. I'm perfectly content." Even to her own ears her declaration sounded hollow.

Dixon pulled out his camera and adjusted the settings. He glanced up at the car roof. "Would you mind opening the sunroof?"

"Why?"

He chuckled. "Why not?"

"Well, because I never do."

"Why not?"

She tried to find a valid reason. Why didn't she use it? During the day it was usually too hot, and she preferred the air conditioning. The one time she had opened it, the wind had blown her hair around. "No particular reason. I just don't."

Dixon shook his finger at her. "Lena, you need to learn to relax. Have fun. Try and enjoy life more."

Lena gritted her teeth. She'd had enough of his teasing. "And you need to try some structure and responsibility. Maybe you should settle down, get married, have a family."

She regretted her words the moment they were spoken and turned to apologize.

Dix was staring out the side window, his jaw flexing rapidly, the muscles in his neck taut. "That's a woman's answer for everything, isn't it? Marriage and family." He ground the words out between clenched teeth. "Well, guess what? Marriage isn't the solution to everything."

Lena flinched at his harsh tone. The intensity of his anger was completely at odds with the man she'd met today. So far he'd been happy-go-lucky and never taken anything seriously. But her comment had hit a raw nerve. Why? What had she said? Was he anti-marriage? Afraid of the commitment necessary?

She stole a glance at Dixon again. He was staring out the window, his hand worrying his chin. No. Dixon Edwards wasn't the kind to avoid commitment. He was too dedicated to his work. He made her uneasy at times, and his methods were irritating, but she didn't doubt that he was a good man.

Lena gripped the steering wheel, waiting for the light to change. So what had upset him?

"Do you like ice cream?"

She stared at her passenger. The old Dix was back. Lighthearted, smiling, and changing directions. Whatever had upset him, he'd gotten over it quickly.

He chuckled softly deep in his throat. "Well, do you?"

"Yes."

"Good. Turn left. I see an ice cream place."

"I can't. I'm in the right-turn lane."

Dixon glanced back over his shoulder. "No one coming. Go for it."

"No." She was not about to break traffic laws so he could get ice cream. "We'll circle the block. Besides, parking for Scoops is in the back. I thought you wanted to take more pictures."

"I do. But I suddenly have a craving for ice cream. So shoot me."

She looked at him, and her heart skipped a beat. He was smiling again, that charming, aren't-I-cute smile that skittered along her nerves. His head was tilted, and his light brown hair fell across his forehead.

"It's green."

"What?"

He nodded toward the street ahead. "The light has changed."

Lena pressed the accelerator too quickly, and the car lunged forward. She regained control and made the turn. *Watch out, Lena. Dix may seem like a nice guy, but it has only been one day. You can't afford to fall for a dimpled smile and a pair of gorgeous blue eyes.*

*Remember Peter. Remember Peter.*

Dixon Edwards took another bite of his ice cream cone and stole a quick glance at Lena, who was walking stiffly at his side, irritated at the delay. His suggestion to stop for a cone had knocked her off balance again. She'd complied, but he knew she wasn't happy at the sudden change in plans.

The suggestion had been a way of apologizing for his foul response to her marriage comment. She had no way of knowing how her words had blindsided him. He'd felt immediately guilty, and he'd been anxious to divert the questions he knew would follow. The ice cream store had been the first place he'd seen.

He chuckled under his breath and took another bite of the birthday-cake-flavored confection. Lena didn't like being directionless. Spontaneity wasn't in her vocabulary. She'd rather be back in her safe, predictable world instead of here with him, not knowing what to expect. He decided to give her a break. "So, is vanilla really your favorite flavor?"

"Yes. But it's vanilla bean."

Dix nodded. "Oh, right. Big difference."

She gave him a disgusted frown and gestured toward the Castillo. "So what part did you want to photograph?"

Dix wondered what she would say if he told her this evening excursion was only partly about work. He did want shots of the fort at night, but he really wanted an excuse to see her again. He'd enjoyed her company today more than any other woman he'd known in a long time.

"I want to catch some shots across the parade ground out to the bay and along this walkway. I think it'll work for the scene near the end." He popped the last bit of cone into his mouth and pulled out his camera. "Go stand there by the chain railing and let me take your picture."

"No."

"Come on, Lena. It'll give the director a better idea of how it'll shoot with the actors in place." Dix knew he should be concentrating on his work, but he was having too much fun teasing her.

She reluctantly agreed, and Dix adjusted the settings on his camera. The Castillo was breathtaking at night. The floodlights cast a golden glow over the area, spilling out onto the bay and reflecting in the still waters. It was the perfect place to film a movie. And the perfect place to be with a lovely woman. He looked through his lens and caught his breath. Lena looked like an angel. The soft light brought out the luminescence of her ivory skin and the delicate planes of her lovely face. He forced himself to concentrate on taking the shots, but the more he saw Lena bathed in the warm glow of the lights, the more he realized he could gaze at her forever.

He took a few more shots of Lena then forced himself to go back to work. Forty-five minutes later, he stowed his gear and joined her at the edge of the seawall. She was staring out at the bay, the breeze gently stirring her dark hair around her face. "It's beautiful here at night. Very romantic, don't you think?"

She shrugged, slipping her hands into the pockets of her jacket. "I suppose."

He looked beyond her to a couple embracing several yards away. "They think so."

Lena turned and looked in the couple's direction. "They're young. They'll learn."

"Learn what?"

She stared into his eyes. "That love can't be counted on."

The sadness in her voice pinched his heart. Dix looked into her green eyes and saw a pain that mirrored his own. For a brief second they understood one another. They'd shared the same disillusionment and heartbreak.

He found himself aching to comfort her, to wrap her in his arms and assure her that she would find love someday. He searched for something to say, but the words he found were either too flippant or too intimate. "He didn't deserve you." A warm flush climbed his neck.

"Who?" Her pretty eyes searched his face.

"The man who broke your heart."

Lena quickly turned away, staring out at the bay. Dix had to restrain himself from pulling her into his arms. The moonlight caressed her hair and spilled onto her shoulders. For a moment he could imagine her like this, at his side forever.

A sobering thought. It was time to take his guide home and focus on his job. He couldn't afford to be distracted by a lovely woman.

## Chapter 3

The Arnez household was bustling with activity when Dix walked in after saying good-night to Lena. He deposited his gear on the bed in his room then started back to the kitchen. He stopped in the doorway, watching the family as they went about their evening routine.

When his old friend Rick Arnez had suggested he stay in his home while scouting locations, Dix had eagerly accepted. It had seemed like the perfect opportunity to work and catch up on old times.

He should have refused. His room was near the living room, and being surrounded by the happy family was harder than he'd anticipated. He turned and walked back into his room, staring out the window to the garden beyond.

He was unusually edgy, restless. And he had no idea why. He had no reason to feel dissatisfied. His life was going well. His business, growing. His ministry, expanding. But part of him wanted something more.

"Would you like some coffee, Dixon?" Kelly called from the kitchen.

Dix ran a hand through his hair and strode back to the family room. "Don't go to any trouble on my account."

"No trouble." She smiled then started the dishwasher. "As soon as I get these kids to bed I'll make a pot. I could use some myself."

"I think I'll go outside and enjoy this weather while I can."

"Good idea. I'm sure the temperatures in Nashville aren't anything like this."

Dix escaped to the deck and the comfort of a deep-cushioned chair where he could think. He hadn't anticipated the internal toll staying with Rick and his family would take. Watching the loving interaction, their happiness, was dredging up emotional silt he'd thought long settled.

He'd come to grips with his situation years ago, and the Father had blessed him beyond measure. He'd found a ministry he loved, one he was passionate about, and it filled his every moment. Or at least it usually did. So what was different now?

Laughter drifted around him from inside the house. Children's laughter. He stood and walked out to the back of the yard, away from the sound. Maybe he should move to a hotel. His budget would take a huge hit, but it might be worth it for the peace of mind.

He turned and glanced at the house next door. Fortunately, his workload would keep him on the road and out of the Arnez home for most of his stay. He also had the perfect guide to show him all the nooks and crannies of St. Augustine. Lena Butler.

"Dixon. Coffee's ready."

He started back toward the house. Lena was going to be a very entertaining and distracting companion. But he had to remember he was here to work. His ministry, bringing the Word to film, took all his time, energy, and devotion.

He walked into the kitchen and found his hosts standing close together. Rick's eyes were filled with love. Dix looked away, a cold knife-edge of sadness slicing across his heart.

There could be no wife or family in his world. And he'd never understand why the Lord had denied him that blessed privilege.

Lena strolled outside to the lanai and eased down onto the glider. Oreo jumped up into her lap. She closed her eyes, savoring the first taste of her morning coffee. Yesterday had been the most unsettling day in recent memory. Dixon Edwards wasn't much different than her first graders—irresponsible, unpredictable, undisciplined.

She'd tried all day to get a handle on him. At first she'd labeled him adolescent, lacking focus, seeing everything as a joke. Yet there had been times at the fort where he'd appeared almost obsessive about his task.

And then there was last night. She'd resented being dragged from her home after dark to take pictures. But standing on the seawall with the warm breeze and the moonlight had forced her to remember how peaceful and soul-soothing the coastline could be.

And how romantic. The reason she never went there anymore. Somehow she'd let her guard slip and allowed Dix to see her old scars.

*He didn't deserve you.*

For a moment she allowed herself to believe he meant it, but then she remembered Dix was a charmer, a man with all the right words at the right times.

Lena took another sip of coffee and glanced over at Kelly's back deck. Movement caught her eye, and she saw Dixon sitting at the patio table. Something about him seemed odd. His elbows were on the table, hands clasped in front of his chin. The hunch of his shoulders suggested worry or distress.

What could make a happy-go-lucky man like Dixon so upset?

Lena told herself to look away, not to intrude upon his privacy, but the image he projected was so far removed from the man she'd met yesterday. She couldn't resist.

Abruptly Dixon stood and walked to the railing around the deck, resting his hands on the top and staring into the distance. After a long while he turned and strode slowly into the house, head bowed as if too heavy to lift.

She didn't realize until he'd disappeared inside that she'd been holding her breath. She thought about his reaction last night to her marriage comment. There had been something dark about him in those moments, as if his flippant attitude hid a great pain. She'd dismissed it as her imagination. Now she wondered.

She rose and went inside for a second cup of coffee. She was being silly. There was nothing deep and mysterious about Dixon Edwards. He was merely a superficial guy who played around with movies. The only thing he understood was having a good time.

So how did she explain that moment last night at the fort when she'd looked into his eyes and felt a connection? When she had the impression that he knew about heartbreak and betrayal on the same deep level as she did?

For one brief second she'd empathized with him. She'd started to ask him to explain, but he'd retreated back into his charming old self, leaving her off balance yet again.

She had a feeling being around Dix would always be unpredictable and surprising. A never-ending adventure. Her secret dream-adventure.

Dix had risen with the sun this morning. Eager to get started on the day's work. Eager to spend time with Lena Butler. He'd called her and moved up their start time by half an hour, which had earned him an irritated sigh through his cell phone. But she hadn't refused. She greeted him at the door with barely concealed irritation and instructions to wait while she finished getting ready.

Her firm teacher tone of voice had suggested she thought he was barely more capable than one of her first graders. He smiled and walked into her living room, frowning at what he found.

For a woman obsessed with organization, this room looked like a stranger lived here. It was a mess. Books stacked in corners, boxes, and bags on the end tables. The fireplace hearth was piled high with CDs and magazines. Mismatched pillows and a variety of throws covered every chair and the sofa.

He glanced back at the kitchen. It looked neat as a pin. So what was up with this room?

Dix moved around slowly, taking in all the items that might reveal something about his guide. The shelves along the far wall were lined with travel books. The movies on the hearth were classics. Off in the corner stood a desk with her computer. The screen saver changed pictures, capturing his attention. He moved closer and smiled. The monitor displayed a picture of Lena standing in front of the Eiffel Tower.

Just as he'd suspected. His little stick-in-the-mud was an adventurer at heart. He chuckled softly. Exactly like his sister. The picture dissolved into one of Lena on the Great

Wall of China. Subsequent photos were from Germany, Moscow, and Hawaii. Something about the pictures bothered him though. He moved in for a closer look.

"I'm ready."

He turned as Lena came into the room. She looked different. "What happened to your glasses?"

She gestured toward her face. "Contacts."

Dix studied her a moment. "You looked good in glasses."

"No one looks good in glasses." Her gaze moved past him to the computer, and she blanched.

He glanced at the screen. "You're quite the world traveler."

Lena turned a nice shade of pink. "Oh, well not really." She came to the desk and shut off the monitor.

"How did you like Nuremberg?" He watched her grow more uncomfortable and decided to give her a break. She was too cute to torment this way. He leaned toward her. "You've never been there, have you?"

A sheepish smile moved her lips. "No. I haven't been to any of those places. My friend edited the photos and put me in them."

Dix laughed and pointed his finger at her. "I knew you were an adventurer at heart. But why make fake pictures? Why not go to these places and take real ones?"

Lena sighed. "I haven't had the time. I've spent the last five years getting my masters and the years before that getting my bachelor's degree."

"What took you so long, if you don't mind me asking?"

"My sisters, Jeanie and Suzanna. Our dad died when I was in my freshman year of college at FSU. My mom had died when I was sixteen, so that left me in charge of the girls. I had to make sure they got their education first. By the time I got them through school, I had to start all over again. I attended Flagler here in town, but only part time."

His heart went out to her. No wonder she was such a control freak. "That's a lot of responsibility for a young woman."

"I was used to it. My mother was sick most of her life, and Dad worked odd hours. Most of the household stuff fell to me."

"So, traveling has been your big dream?"

"Yes. Maybe someday I'll get to see some of those places for myself."

"Which one would you go to first?"

"China."

He smiled at how quickly she'd responded. "Why?"

"I want to stand on the Great Wall. It must be an awe-inspiring sight."

"It is."

"You've been there?"

Dix nodded, noting how her green eyes sparkled with excitement. She really was very pretty. She only needed to ease up a bit and learn to enjoy life more. "It's phenomenal. Everywhere you look, it's there. Over every hill, crest, rise. Standing on it leaves you in awe of its age and size." Lena smiled, and Dix's heart skipped a beat. He'd better be careful. He was starting to like his guide. Teasing her was entertaining, but he shouldn't get too entangled.

"Maybe someday I'll be able to go. If I get this promotion, I'll be able to afford to travel."

"Oh yes, the promotion. So let me ask you, is security worth giving up something you love?"

"I'm a single woman. I have to think of my future. I don't have a husband to take care of me." Lena turned and rifled through her stack of papers. "I made a list of places to check out today that might meet your needs. I have the list here someplace."

Dix chuckled and gestured at the messy stacks of paper on her desk. "How would you know?"

Lena glared over her shoulder. "I have a system. I know where everything is."

Dix tugged at his ear. "For someone so fond of organization and responsibility, your own office is a bit"—he searched for a nice word—"cluttered."

Lena pulled two sheets of paper from the mess and attached them to the clipboard. "I don't like paperwork."

Dix frowned, following her out of the room. "Then why are you so anxious to get the vice principal's job? Won't that mean more paperwork?"

"Probably. But it'll be worth it."

"Right. The security."

Lena pulled the back door closed behind them and started toward the car. "I wouldn't expect you to understand."

"Why?"

"Anyone who would give up a perfectly secure job like owning a marketing company to make movies has no concept of security."

Dix smiled at her prim little walk. It didn't match the cute figure he was admiring at the moment. She wore dark khaki, cropped pants that revealed a pair of shapely calves and dainty feet inside brightly beaded sandals. Her lime green knit top highlighted her tan and the rich coffee color of her hair. He corralled his wayward thoughts. "Define it."

"What?"

Dix slid into the front seat of Lena's car and buckled up. "Define security. What is it? How do you get it, and how can you be sure that it won't go away?"

Lena flashed him an irritated scowl. "I know nothing is

completely secure but our salvation. But I also know I have
to do my part to make my life as secure as I possibly can."

"I agree."

"You do?"

Dix nodded. "But I don't agree that you should put your
dreams and your life on hold to obtain that security. When
you do that, you're basing your future on fear, depending
on your own strength and abilities to protect you. What
about the Father's place in your life?"

She cranked the car to life. "I know He's in control, but
He expects me to do my part as well. I knew you wouldn't
understand." She backed out of the driveway. "Where do
you want to start today?"

"Let's find a dark alley." Dix hid the smile that came to
his lips. He loved watching Lena's expressive face whenever he threw her a curve. First she'd get wide-eyed. Then
she'd blink. Then her lips would part slightly, and she'd
exhale a little huff of air. Next would come the darkening
eyes, the tight lips, and sometimes the hands on the hips.

"What are you talking about?"

"I need to find an alley that opens onto a courtyard with
a restaurant beside it for scene twenty-eight."

Lena set her jaw and put the car in Drive. "I hate it when
you change topics so abruptly."

"I know."

Dix turned and smiled out the window. It was going to
be an interesting week.

The afternoon temperatures were rising. Even in the
sheltered courtyard of the Blue Waves Bed and Breakfast,
the heat was becoming uncomfortable. She and Dix had
come to the old home in the historic section of St. Augustine to search out a possible site on his list.

Lena sat in the fifties-style glider beneath giant crepe

myrtle trees, watching Dix talk with the owners. The man didn't know a stranger. He could strike up a conversation with anyone about anything—and had done so the entire morning. Part of her envied his ease with strangers. She normally chose to avoid interaction with others and go about her business.

Dix had given her the lead again, and she'd decided to take him at his word and visit her favorite places. They'd toured the Old City Gates, the Oldest House, and the Lightner Museum. She'd regaled him with all the historic data she knew, and he seemed genuinely interested. But she could never be sure with him. At times he'd seemed preoccupied, but she reminded herself that he was working, no matter how it might look to her.

He'd been ruthless with his camera today, insisting that she be in many of the photos so he could get a feel for how the shots would look in the film.

It was all a waste of time in her opinion, but at least she was spending this beautiful day enjoying her city. Though it was hot today, unseasonably humid. A front was moving through later, and rain was due during the night.

She smiled and closed her eyes, inhaling the heady mix of fragrances that drenched the air this time of year. It was a perfect day. Almost. She looked over at Dix, who was shaking hands with a man she'd never seen before. While she'd been daydreaming, the bed-and-breakfast owner had left and another man had taken his place.

Keeping up with Dix was a full-time job. She glanced at her watch then at the list of locations still to be secured. At this rate Dix would never find them all. He really needed to be more organized.

She looked over at him, and he smiled and winked. Her heart did a funny skip in her chest. She had to admit he was an attractive man. She'd be lying if she said otherwise. But attractiveness didn't mean anything. Lots of men were handsome.

To be fair, Dix had been nothing but kind and gentlemanly since they'd met. He'd never made a crude comment or an inappropriate gesture. While his attitude was always flippant and flirtatious, he was never out of line. But that didn't mean she could let her guard down. A charmer was still a charmer, and she'd never make that mistake again.

"Scratch another one off our list." Dix came and sat down beside her. "What's next, boss?"

Lena rolled her eyes. He'd taken to calling her that for some reason. "There's a park nearby that has a pavilion, and the next street over has a small grocery store."

"Let's go." He stood and exhaled slowly. "Man, it's hot today."

"It's Florida." He was right. The temperature and the humidity were rising. She waved the clipboard in front of her face a few times, enjoying the small breeze.

Dix stopped and looked at her.

"What?"

"Wait right there. I'll be back." He jogged off toward a small shop down the street and disappeared inside.

Lena checked her watch again. Apparently location scouting had no time limits. If only he would focus on one task until it was completed.

Dix reappeared, hurrying toward her, a huge smile on his face. "I got you something." He handed her a tiny battery-operated fan on a string.

"What is this for?"

He took it from her, draped it over her neck, then turned it on. A gentle breeze blew against her neck and chin.

"That'll keep you cool while we walk today." He pointed to the label on the back. "And it's made in China."

Her first impulse was to give it back and scold him for

being childish. But the smile on his face wouldn't allow it. He looked like a little boy who'd picked a flower especially for his mother. The more she thought about it, the more the humor of his gesture struck her. The giggle erupted from her throat before she could stop it. "You're crazy, you know that?"

"So they tell me."

As they walked toward the park Lena couldn't help but notice how comfortable she'd become with him at her side. For all his haphazard ways, he did make a person feel special. Trouble was, he made everyone feel that way. She wanted to feel special to one particular person. "So was the B & B owner excited about possibly being in your movie?"

"No. He refused permission."

"Why? I would think it would be free publicity for them. Why wouldn't he want that?"

Dix looked down at her. His blue eyes held a hint of sadness. "He didn't want to be associated with a Christian film."

It took a second to process his words. "Oh. That never occurred to me. I mean, I assumed everyone would want to have their business in a movie."

"It happens." Dix explained further as they waited to cross the street. "Sometimes they don't want to close their businesses for the shoot, even though they're well compensated. A lot of people are leery of the movie business and feel that they're going to be cheated somehow."

"Who was the other man I saw you with?"

"He's the pastor of a small church in the suburbs. He offered to let us shoot there if we wanted. We may check it out later this week."

Lena stopped inside the small park and turned off her tiny fan. It was cooler here under the giant live oaks. "There's an old bench over there that might work for scene 104."

Dix glanced around the park. "This is incredible."

Lena nodded and checked her list. "Yes. It is. Do you want to see about the bench or would you rather see if that pavilion is good?"

Dix turned and pinned her with his blue eyes. "Are you seeing this, Lena?"

"Yes, Dix. I've seen it a dozen times before."

"No. I mean here, right now, at this precise moment."

"Yes." Sometimes, Dix's charm grew tiresome.

He took the clipboard from her and dropped it on the ground. Then he grasped her shoulders and turned her to face the park. "I want you to stop and really see this place, Lena. Look at those flowers, the vibrant color, the vivid foliage. See the blue sky peeking through the trees overhead. Now close your eyes and inhale that fragrant breeze. Let it get deep down inside you so you'll never forget it."

His hands gently squeezed her shoulders, and he stepped closer. She could feel his chest against her back. The warmth of his body made her tremble.

"Now, listen." He spoke softly against her hair.

She froze. All she could hear was the beating of her own heart and the sudden rush of blood pounding in her ears. But she did as he asked and focused on the birds overhead. At first she only heard a loud complaining jay, but soon she could detect other songbirds and the gulls from the shore. Pigeons cooed.

"Now open your eyes again, and pretend you're a camera and take a mental picture, Lena. Be in the moment. Capture every detail so you can come back next week, or next year, and not only remember this moment but relive it. Don't let anything else intrude."

Lena stared at the park scene in front of her. She could hear not only the birds but the leaves rustling in the trees, the *clip-clop* of a horse-drawn carriage on the next street, a car horn, voices, a million things. The breeze danced against her skin, stirring her pants against her legs and strands of hair against her cheek.

Her gaze landed on the dark, rough texture of the live oaks with their thick branches drooping nearly to the ground. Spanish moss, luxurious and lacy, draped like jewelry from every branch. The azaleas had never been so beautiful. The bougainvillea so full. She smiled. She'd never seen the park this way before and never would again.

She turned to tell Dix as the breeze wafted around them, encasing her in his scent and weakening her knees. It would be so easy to turn and rest her head against his chest. To add him to the indelible picture she'd just taken.

Stunned at the direction of her thoughts, Lena straightened and stepped away. "We'd better get back to work. We have a lot to do." She picked up the clipboard and hurriedly scanned the sheets. She had a feeling she'd ruined something special, but Dixon Edwards was more dangerous than she ever suspected.

## Chapter 4

Dixon stole a glance at Lena as they strolled along the pathway. They'd driven over to the lighthouse after lunch, but she'd been quiet and withdrawn since they'd left the restaurant. No. Come to think of it, she'd been distant since he'd forced her to take a closer look at the park. Maybe he shouldn't have been so overbearing about that. He had to remember Lena, like his sister, was resistant to change. He couldn't push her too hard or too quickly. "I got some great shots from the top of the lighthouse. Thanks for climbing up there with me." He adjusted the setting on his camera from stills to video. "We're making good progress on these locations. You're an excellent guide. I couldn't have done this without you."

Lena chuckled. "Yes you could. There's any number of people here who could show you around."

"None as attractive." He braced, unsure of how she'd

react to his compliment. Denise had socked him the first time he'd given her one. But then, sisters did that.

She frowned and looked at the clipboard. "You need some warehouses and a rural road. We could drive out toward Hastings later today if you'd like."

"Good idea. Can we open the sunroof?" His comment earned him a smile. She really had a sweet smile. He didn't think he'd ever get tired of seeing it.

"Can I ask you a question?" Lena said as they strolled toward the parking lot.

"Shoot."

"Why movies?"

"It was either that or graduate seminary."

"You went to seminary?"

He tried not to laugh at the shock in her green eyes. "I started. But that's where I saw my first Christian film, and I knew right away what I wanted to do."

"But wouldn't completing your training have been more productive? Think of the people you could have ministered to."

"Not if that wasn't what God really wanted me to do. I can reach five times the amount of people with a film than with a pulpit."

"I know, but—"

"That security thing keeps bothering you, doesn't it?" She nodded. "It's important to me."

"Why?" He stopped beside the car, forcing her to do the same and face him. "Why is having everything planned out ahead of time so imperative?"

Lena crossed her arms over her chest and stared at the ground as if searching for a place to begin. "My dad was in sales. He changed jobs a lot. Always looking for a better opportunity. We never knew from week to week if we'd eat hot dogs or steak or if the power bills would get paid or not. That's a horrible way to live."

"I'm sure it was. But he must have done pretty well for the family. You had a roof over your head. An education."

"I worked my way through college, and I helped my sisters. Our dad wasn't around much. He spent more time thinking about himself than his daughters."

"What about your mom?"

Lena stiffened. "Mom was an alcoholic." She turned and walked off a few paces.

Dix followed, his heart going out to her. He touched her back lightly to let her know he was there. "My granddad was an alcoholic. He lived with us. I never knew which grandpa would be there when I got home from school each day. The happy-go-lucky one or the angry, violent one."

Lena turned and looked at him, her green eyes reflecting her surprise and a hint of gratitude. He knew the look. It was always comforting to learn someone else understood your pain and shame.

"It makes you crave security."

"Or realize there's no such thing." Dix watched her expression as the idea took root in her mind. If she was anything like him, and most people, she had a hard time accepting that any part of life was out of her control.

He'd been a Christian since he was a child, but he'd never fully understood the tenets of trusting the Lord and giving his life completely to Him until he'd been faced with his own life-changing moment.

He wished he could prevent Lena from learning that lesson the hard way, but he expected her belief in her own ability to provide security was deep-rooted. Only the Lord could work through that fear with her.

"Would you like to call it a day?"

She shook her head. "We have too much to do yet. Where to next?"

"Miss Butler!"

Lena turned around as two little girls ran toward her.

The change that came over his guide captivated Dix. She'd gone from somber and thoughtful to animated and smiling.

Lena stooped down to greet the children, opening her arms to embrace them. They looked to be about four years old. Twins. The mother and an older woman followed a few steps behind.

"Hello, girls. What a nice surprise. What are you doing today?"

"Our grandma is coming to our house," one announced happily.

"We're 'sploring," the other explained seriously.

"What fun. I love to explore." She glanced up at the women. "Hello, Mrs. Williams."

"Good to see you. I'd like you to meet my mother, Mrs. Newton. Mom, Miss Butler is the girls' Sunday school teacher."

Lena stood and shook hands. "Nice to meet you. This is Dixon Edwards."

The mother's smiled widened. "We know who you are. The moviemaker. We're so excited that you're going to be filming here in St. Augustine. How soon will you start?"

"Not until next year. I'm only scouting locations this trip." Dix chatted with the women but was distracted by the interaction between Lena and the little girls. They were talking and giggling happily. He'd never considered Lena a beauty. Cute, yes. Attractive, but at the moment, with these children, she positively glowed with happiness.

A strange tightness formed in his chest, making it hard to breathe. For the first time since he'd made his arrangement with Lena, he wondered if he'd made a huge mistake. Staying with Rick and his family was proving to be problematic. Getting too close to a woman like Lena Butler could prove disastrous. She was a forever kind of woman. The type who would expect a life he couldn't give her.

Lena glanced over at Dix beside her in the passenger seat. He'd been unusually quiet and thoughtful since they'd left the light station. The only other time she'd seen him so somber was that morning on Kelly's deck when he'd looked so dejected. She searched for something to say that would draw him out. "I think I know where you can find that window with a view of a hospital."

Dix looked up. "Oh?"

"We can check it out after we find the fountains."

"Good."

Maybe a change of topic might stir him to conversation. "Weren't the girls cute? I'll hate to see them go this year."

"Where are they going?"

"They'll move up to the next grade."

Dix stared at her a long moment. She couldn't read his expression. Assessing perhaps.

"You teach Sunday school, too?"

"Yes."

"You really enjoy kids, don't you?"

"I do."

"You never wanted children of your own?"

Lena gripped the steering wheel and shook her head. "I told you. I feel like I raised my two younger sisters. I'm in no hurry to raise any more. One family a lifetime is plenty. I have my students and my church kids. That's sufficient."

Dix nodded. "I hear you. I'm too busy with my ministry to have time for a family. Making movies is an all-consuming profession."

"You really believe in the Christian film business, don't you?"

"I do. I know some people don't understand. They think a calling should be to the pulpit or to inner-city work or foreign missions. But we can't all do that. There are so many ways to spread His light. Film has the most untapped potential. People love movies. Not just in theaters, but they're watching them online now, having them sent to their mailboxes.

"Films become part of the culture, of our psyches. They evoke feelings and memories we keep all our lives. We quote our favorite lines until they become part of our vocabulary."

Dix shifted in his seat, leaning forward to catch her gaze. "Think what we could do with a godly film. Dialogue based on the Word. What if scripture rolled off people's tongues like their favorite movies' lines, only impacting them much deeper, changing their hearts and minds."

"It would be wonderful, but I guess I don't see that happening. People only want graphic images in films."

Dix shook his head. "Look at the Christian music industry, Lena. It's grown into a huge business, rivaling the secular markets. Christian fiction is the fastest growing segment of publishing today. I want Christian films to be that way, too. I want the theaters to be filled with them. Even more, I want the movies to be so good that the word *Christian* doesn't even come into play. People will come because the stories are uplifting, inspiring, and speak the truth."

Lena parked the car in the visitors' lot at Flagler College and turned to Dix. His blue eyes were bright with enthusiasm, and his white teeth flashed in his smile. She couldn't help but smile back.

Dix shrugged. "Sorry. I get carried away."

"I think I may have short-changed you, Dix. I didn't realize how much passion you bring to your work. I can see where there would be little room for a permanent relationship."

His smile faded, and a brief sadness flashed through his eyes. "Women like to be first in a man's life." He rested one hand on the dash. "They want permanence, kids, dog, the whole nine yards. That's not for me. I couldn't pull that off and still do my work."

"I know. I devote all my time to my students and my church. I wouldn't have time to fit in a relationship if I wanted to. I guess some people aren't meant to be a couple."

Dixon Edwards finished the e-mail to his partner and hit the Send button. He leaned back in his desk chair, listening to the rain splatter on the bedroom window. He'd been trying to work since Lena had dropped him off after grabbing a quick burger earlier this evening. He needed to look through his photos and scene lists to assess his progress, but concentrating on his job was impossible. He couldn't keep his thoughts from drifting to Lena.

Dix punched a few keys and pulled up the images he'd taken today, smiling at the ones he'd shot of his delightful guide. She'd no idea he'd been taking her picture. The candid moments captured her personality completely. The perfectly creased pants, the crisp top, and her always-straight posture.

Dixon enlarged the one he'd taken of Lena staring out at the water from the gun deck of the fort. Her expression was one of longing and anticipation, as if she were waiting for something wonderful to appear on the horizon.

His heart beat a little faster in his chest. Lena wasn't interested in having a family.

A small ray of hope had been born in him that moment. Lena was a woman he could easily love. He might be falling for her already. He'd resisted the feelings, reminding himself his ministry was and always would be foremost in his life. He'd given up everything for it. He'd offered himself completely to the Lord. All his talents, his abilities, and his heart.

But there was still a part of his heart he'd reserved for that one special woman. He'd never expected to find her. Not with his limitations. But maybe Lena was the one in a million he could plan a future with.

A small sting touched his conscience. He hadn't intended to lie to Lena about not wanting a permanent relationship, but he realized the moment he'd said the words that he wasn't being honest, with her or himself. He did want a relationship, a wife, a family. But the Lord had set him on a path, and he'd vowed to be obedient. His heart, however, was yearning for something more. Until now he'd rarely thought about his situation. He and his business partner, Larry, had poured their hearts and souls into creating and growing their company.

Traveling kept him too preoccupied to be distracted by anything or anyone. St. Augustine had exposed a part of himself he didn't know existed. A part he'd thought he'd come to terms with. Now he wondered if all he'd done was push it into the recesses of his mind instead of dealing with it head-on.

He picked up a pen and scribbled a note to himself to search out places in his Bible that dealt with avoidance. It might be time for a spiritual checkup.

His gaze drifted back to the image of Lena on his screen. He shouldn't get ahead of himself. Lena was a woman bent on security, even if she secretly longed for the adventure he could give her. Convincing her to uproot and change directions would be a nearly impossible job.

Unless God was on his side.

*"You do not have because you do not ask."*

Dix rubbed his forehead. *Well, Father, I'm asking.*

Lena stood on the threshold of the back door, watching the rain outside the lanai. It was a nice steady downpour, the perfect spring rain. Nice and steady. Why did the words bring Dixon Edwards to mind?

He was a nice man. Steady seemed an odd word to describe him, but in some ways, he was steady. For all his carefree approach to life and his manner, there was something very grounded about Dix.

She kept replaying his comments about not having time for a wife and family. Something about his declaration nagged at the back of her mind. Why would a gregarious soul like Dixon not want a family? He would be a fantastic father.

Lena turned away from the rain show, walked back through the kitchen into the living room, and curled up on the couch. Oreo joined her. She sighed. She understood Dixon's devotion to his work. Teaching took all her energy. All her time. She'd be forty in a few years. Marriage wasn't a likely scenario. True, it was a new millennium, and women were marrying later and bearing children well into their fifties. But for her, family wasn't a likely option.

She didn't date. She didn't socialize outside of school and church. She rarely met eligible men. So what did that leave? Dixon Edwards? Hardly. Nice or not, he wasn't the kind of man she'd plan a future with.

So why did her heart refuse to behave when he was around? And why did he invade her thoughts even when she was determined to keep him out?

Charm. She was susceptible to his charm, and it was time she got control of herself before something disastrous happened.

"Come in." Lena fastened the elastic band around her hair to keep it at the back of her neck and walked toward her desk. Dix was here, and she was anxious to have a few words with him this morning. She'd had all she could take of his disorganized approach to his job.

He strode into the living room, rubbing his hands together expectantly, a smile lighting his blue eyes and exposing his dimple. "Ready to rock and roll?"

Lena ignored the energy Dix always brought with him. It was time to corral some of that and redirect it. "We're not going anywhere yet." She held up the clipboard.

"Yet?"

His smile faded so quickly she wanted to laugh. But this was no joking matter. "I can't take another day of your haphazard approach to this job. It wastes time, and it's unproductive. At this rate you'll still be scouting locations when the movie starts filming."

"What would you suggest?"

"I'm going to take these sheets of yours and reorganize them."

Dix frowned. "They are organized."

"Not logically." She held out her hand. "I assume you have this on a flash drive or something?"

Dix pulled the small silver drive from his pocket and handed it to her. "I thought you didn't like paperwork."

"This isn't paperwork. This is organization. That's different."

"How?"

Lena sat down at her computer and inserted the device.

Dix pointed over her shoulder to the correct file. "Paper-work is boring. Organizing is fun."

She took a few moments to grasp his format then made her changes. She hit the Print button and pulled out the flash drive, handing it back to Dix. "Okay. Try this." She pulled the sheets off the printer and handed them to him.

Dix looked it over, a deep crease in his forehead. "It's all listed by location instead of scene."

"Exactly." Lena crossed her arms over her chest. "Now we can find similar sites, take all the pictures we need, then move on to the next. No more bouncing around from downtown street to country road and back again. This way we'll find all the downtown locations then move out to the suburbs or to the beach."

Dix rubbed the back of his neck. "I don't know. Tina organized these sheets herself, though she has her own quirky way of doing things. I still need to look at each scene to see if I've got every shot covered. What if I miss something?"

"We can reset the parameters at the end of each day so you can double check according to scene. At least this way we aren't driving helter-skelter all over the place."

"We'll give it a try. As long as Tina gets what she needs."

"I'm sure it will work." Lena stood and walked into the kitchen. "Do you realize we passed dozens of locations that matched your criteria? You were so focused on one par-ticular site that you completely missed the opportunity."

Dix smiled, stopping beside her at the counter. "You're very good at this. Have you ever thought about doing this for a living?"

Lena turned off the coffeemaker. "Don't be ridiculous."

"I'm serious, Lena. We work well together. You could

throw over this administrative gig and come to work for me."

For a fraction of a second, Lena actually entertained the outlandish idea. Common sense returned quickly. "No thank you. I have a job. I'm a teacher." She started to move, but Dix stepped in front of her, an impish grin on his face.

"That doesn't mean you can't change careers. I'm happier now than when I was a marketing exec. Happier than if I'd gone into the pulpit. Maybe you'd be happier doing something completely different."

"I doubt it." She stepped around him and slipped her cell into her purse.

"Think about it, Lena." His voice was laced with excitement. "We could travel all over the country—the world, for that matter. I'm always going someplace. Either for meetings with backers or research. It's something all the time. That's why I love the job so much." He took her arm and pulled her around to face him. "You can't tell me the idea doesn't excite you. I know you long for adventure. To see all the famous sights of the world. Come to work for me, and you can have everything you ever wanted."

Lena looked into his clear blue eyes, her heart fluttering. With one word she could achieve her dreams. Travel. Adventure. Freedom from burdensome responsibility.

What was wrong with her? She had to be out of her mind. She grabbed her purse. "We'd better get busy."

Dix followed slowly behind. "So where do we start, O Fearless Leader?"

Lena climbed into the driver's seat, cranking the engine as soon as Dix settled in the car. "You've got several rural locations to track down. They're more general in nature, so we can knock those out in a few hours then tackle the more specific sites in town this afternoon."

Lena inhaled a deep, contented breath as she pulled out

onto Inlet Drive. At least today would be more productive. Now that she was in charge, Dix's location search should be completed in half the time. Maybe he'd even finish in time for her to salvage some of her spring break. She really had been looking forward to transplanting those cannas.

At least, she had been.

Dixon stared at the central Florida landscape as it sped by the car window. He was used to the rolling hills of Nashville. The flat, lush farmland here was a fascinating change. Grass and produce farms spread out as far as the eye could see, broken now and then by a nursery filled with flowers.

The view could only distract him briefly. He was still kicking himself for his lapse of common sense earlier. He hadn't intended to offer Lena a job, but once the idea had entered his head he'd warmed to it. He watched her eyes as she digested his invitation, and he'd known the moment she decided against it. His disappointment was more than he'd expected. It was time he stepped back and regained his perspective. He was here to work, and Lena Butler was here to assist him. Period.

He smiled over at his companion, tapping his pen against the clipboard. "I have to admit, Lena, your system works pretty well. I think we've found twice as many sites as we would have with my list."

Lena rewarded him with a smile. "You're welcome."

A surge of affection engulfed him as he watched her drive. It had been a good morning. He'd enjoyed being with her, even more than yesterday. She was the perfect companion. She'd even been less rigid today, probably because she felt she was in control. But still, he'd seen a change in her that he liked.

He studied her a moment. In fact, a change he wanted to push a little bit. "We need to find a helicopter service."

"What? Why?"

Dix smiled inwardly. Good going. She flinched at his unexpected request, but she hadn't displayed her usual wide-eyed shock. Merely normal curiosity. Maybe his little control freak was starting to change. "I think I'd like to take a look at the city from the air."

"I didn't see any aerial shots on the sheets."

"There aren't. This is for me. I need an overall sense of direction. I think I can get that best from the air."

She thought a moment before answering. "Then we'd better head to the airport."

"In Jacksonville?"

"No. The regional airport here. We don't have commercial service to St. Augustine any longer. Only private flights and helicopters."

"Do you know anyone in the business?"

"Sorry. No."

Dix pulled up the needed information on his smartphone and sorted through the tour businesses. "How about Eagles Wings Tours. Sounds biblical."

The office of the helicopter tour company wasn't difficult to find. Dix held the door for Lena to enter.

A tall, well-built man with dark hair and brown eyes greeted them. "Good afternoon. I'm Zach Montgomery. Can I help you?"

"I hope so. I'm Dixon Edwards. This is my assistant, Lena Butler."

Montgomery shook hands. "Butler. Of course. We went to school together. You were a year ahead of me."

Lena smiled. "Yes, I was. Nice to see you again."

"You're Jeanie Butler's sister, aren't you?"

Lena nodded. "Yes I am."

"What can I help you with?"

Dix nodded toward the clipboard in Lena's hands. "I'm scouting locations for a movie to be filmed here, and I need an aerial perspective. Think you can help?"

"Absolutely. When do you want to go?"

Dix glanced briefly at Lena before he replied. "How about now?"

Montgomery nodded thoughtfully. "Well, I'll need a half hour or so to prepare, but yeah, we can go do that."

"Oh, I'm also going to need an aerial photographer."

Zach nodded, resting his hands on his hips. "I don't offer that service through my company, but I have a buddy who does that kind of work. You need him today?"

"No. But probably within the next few weeks."

"I'll have him get in touch with you."

Dix handed him a card. "That would be great. Thanks."

Dix's stomach growled, and he realized they hadn't eaten since morning. He looked at Lena. "How about we go grab a bite to eat and come back in forty-five minutes or so?"

"That'll work." Zach gestured toward the woman seated behind the desk across the small room. "The Fly-By Café at the airport has great food. Vivian will take care of your charges and answer any questions you might have. I'll see you back here shortly."

When they returned to the office after lunch, Dix had formulated a plan. He had little hope that it would work, but he was eager to try. He spied Montgomery standing near a bright yellow chopper and steered Lena in that direction.

"We're ready to go." Zach opened the door to the aircraft.

Dix took Lena's hand and started forward. "This should be fun. Have you ever been in a chopper before?"

Lena's eyes grew wide, and she stopped, pulling her hand from his. "I'm not going up in that thing. I'll wait for you right here on the ground."

Zach glanced back at them, but Dix gestured for him to wait a moment. "Lena, don't let your obsession about control rob you of a new experience."

"I'm not. I just don't want to die."

Dix chuckled. "You're not going to die. This guy does this every day. Besides, you saw the cross on his logo. The man's obviously a Christian, and you know what that means."

"What?"

"The Father's his co-pilot." Lena glanced at the chopper, and Dix could see her deeply buried longing for adventure starting to surface in her green eyes. Part of her wanted to fly. But was that part strong enough yet to push aside her need for safety and security in all its forms? "Think of it this way," he urged gently. "You can have the adventure you've always wanted and never leave St. Augustine."

"But I'll be leaving the ground."

Dix laughed. This woman was the most enchanting he'd ever known. "Come on, Lena. I'll be with you. Right at your side." She glanced at the copter again, and he could sense her weakening. He pointed to the pilot waiting patiently beside the craft. "Look at him. A big, strong, handsome man. A skilled pilot. He inspires confidence in me. What about you?"

"He's not *that* handsome."

Zach snickered then feigned being insulted.

"Come on. Let's live dangerously for once." Dix held out his hand and was thrilled and surprised when she gave him hers. Her trust in him overwhelmed him and filled him with an unexpected surge of protectiveness. He wanted to keep her safe, to make sure nothing bad ever shadowed her life.

But as they walked toward the helicopter to begin their adventure, another thought formed in his mind. Lena may be letting go of her defenses, but his own were dropping as well, and that wasn't good. Maybe it was time to put some distance between them. The idea made him sad and a bit angry, but his life was what it was. Only the Lord could change it, and He'd seen fit not to do that.

As soon as the chopper landed, he'd have to put some serious distance between himself and the charming Lena Clare.

The pilot climbed aboard, and Dix opened the front passenger-side door. He looked at Lena and tried to hide his amusement. She was wide-eyed and chewing her lip. "You want to ride up front? You have the best view from there."

"No. The back. Are you riding up front?"

Dix wanted to hug her. She looked so adorable. Like a little girl afraid of her first pony ride. "Why don't we both ride in the back?"

"Won't you be able to see better up there with Zach?"

A rush of affection warmed his veins. Lena couldn't help thinking of others first. "I'll have a perfect view from back here." Dix helped her in and climbed in behind her, then helped her adjust her headphones and seat belt.

"Y'all ready back there?" Zach glanced over his shoulder and spoke through the headset.

Dix gave a thumbs-up. "Off we go." He glanced at Lena. She was sitting straight as a board in the seat, hands clasped so tightly in her lap her knuckles were turning white.

The rotor gained momentum, and the cockpit started to

vibrate slightly. The noise level rose, reverberating in his chest, but the headset kept the interior levels quiet.

Zach spoke to the tower, rattling off flight information. Dix kept his eyes on Lena. The chopper rose into the air, pushing them down into their seats. Lena gasped and stiffened. The copter floated a moment, then moved forward.

Zach turned his head toward the back. "Nothing to worry about, folks. A swing and sway is normal at liftoff. We'll settle down to a nice, easy flight real soon. Just sit back and relax. Mr. Edwards, you want a running commentary as we travel, or are you familiar with the area?"

"Talk it up, Captain. This is my first trip to St. Augustine. And the name is Dix."

"Copy that, Dix."

Lena looked over at him, her face pale, her lips folded together. He wanted her to enjoy this ride and not be terrified. If she would relax, he was convinced she'd love the view of her beloved hometown from the air. He reached over and pried her fingers loose from one another and took hold of her hand. She resisted then held on, sending him a grateful smile.

The aircraft rose and dipped to the right. Lena held tight to his hand, and he sent her a reassuring smile. Zach began his spiel, and Dix felt Lena relax a bit. Within a few moments she was leaning toward the side window, peering down at the spectacular view of St. Augustine. Her excitement was contagious. Her dreamy smile set off little bursts of affection inside his chest.

Dix knew he should be focusing on the sights himself, but he couldn't take his eyes off Lena. By the time they touched down again, all her fears had vanished, and she was bubbling with happiness.

After saying good-bye to Zach, they headed back across the tarmac to the car. Lena gently touched his arm.

"Thank you."

He smiled down at her. "For what?"

"For not letting me back out. I would have missed a truly wonderful adventure."

Dix stopped and looked into her eyes. He wanted nothing more in this moment than to lay the world at her feet. To take her hand and fulfill every dream she'd ever had.

Every dream he'd had as well.

"My pleasure, Sunshine."

# Chapter 5

Lena pulled to a stop in the Grace Community Church parking lot as dusk was settling in. She allowed herself a moment to enjoy the gentle breeze swirling in from the open sunroof.

She'd been noticing her surroundings a lot more this week. Reconnecting with small pleasures she'd put aside in her quest for her degree and future security.

She closed her eyes, grinning gleefully as she thought about the day's events. She'd flown in a helicopter. She still couldn't believe she'd actually done it. Never in her wildest dreams would she have even considered taking such a risk. But somehow, Dixon Edwards had convinced her to let go of her fears and experience a new adventure.

She was so glad she'd listened. The flight had been more than she'd ever imagined. Exhilarating. Amazing. The scenery from above had taken her breath away. Her beloved old city was as enchanting from the air as on the ground.

And completing the picture had been Dix's contagious enthusiasm. His passion and joy had eased her fears, keeping her attention on the sights below and not the fact that she was in the air.

And he'd called her Sunshine.

Her heart skipped a beat, and her blood warmed at the memory. A nickname. She'd never had one before. She liked it. And she liked the way she felt when she was with Dix. She shouldn't though. It was dangerous.

Dixon was a charming man, and she was susceptible to his type. How could she ever trust herself with a man like him again? Especially when he offered her the dream of her life—a life of adventure.

For a moment she'd thought he was serious when he'd suggested she come to work for him, and she'd actually let herself imagine it. Then she'd remembered she was changing jobs. She was leaving teaching and going into administration. That was enough adventure for now. But Dix hadn't mentioned it again. In fact, he'd begged off further scouting when they'd returned home late this afternoon.

It was just as well. She was behind on her errands, and she had to pick up her Sunday school supplies before the office closed for the day. After picking up her materials from the Christian education director, Lena stepped across the hall to the church office to speak to Kelly. Her friend had taken over the job of bookkeeper a year ago.

"How are you enjoying your time without children?" Kelly's mom had taken the two girls home with her for a few days.

Kelly looked up from her computer and smiled. "Hi, Lena. Rick and I are thoroughly enjoying the quiet time.

We've been to a movie, out to dinner, and I think we're going to a concert tomorrow night."

"Too bad you have a houseguest."

"Dix? We hardly see him." Kelly rose and gathered up a few folders. "How's the location hunt going?"

"Good. Would you believe he got me into a helicopter today?"

Kelly's mouth gaped. "No way."

Lena nodded, unable to keep from grinning. "I know. It shocked me, too."

"I knew he'd be good for you."

"Now don't go jumping to conclusions."

Kelly wagged a finger. "You like him. Don't try and deny it."

"I won't. He's nice. But I've only known him three days."

"Plenty of time. Oh, by the way, Mrs. Watson made a sizeable contribution to his ministry. And I do mean sizeable."

Lena's stomach knotted. "Really? What brought that on?"

Kelly shrugged. "Seems she saw one of his promotional films and decided that she wanted to further his cause."

The sense of joy she'd felt all afternoon faded. "Has he been asking for donations?"

"No. Not that I'm aware. Why?"

Lena shrugged. "Mrs. Watson is known to be rather frugal."

Kelly chuckled softly. "Tight, you mean. I guess he got to her."

Lena set her jaw. "That's what I'm afraid of."

"What do you mean?"

Too late Lena remembered that Dixon Edwards was a close friend of Rick's and a houseguest of Kelly's. Questioning his motives and his character was rude and unkind. "Nothing, really. It's odd though, that she should suddenly give money to someone she hardly knows."

"I give money to people I don't know all the time, Lena. So do you. I donate to school projects, give love offerings at concerts, and drop money in the bins at Christmastime."

"I suppose you're right."

The news of Mrs. Watson's donation nagged at Lena as she walked over to the fellowship center for the family night supper. Dix hadn't actually solicited donations, but he'd jokingly suggested that money was always a good way to keep Christian films in production.

Peter had solicited donations. Funds that had been given in good faith. Funds he had absconded with in the dead of night.

She didn't want to put Dix in the same category as Peter, but it was hard to quell her suspicions. She'd been burned too badly, and she'd sworn she'd never let herself be blinded again. Yet here she was, fighting the pull of attraction for Dixon Edwards, a man who could easily be another Peter Cane.

Her conscience stung. She didn't honestly believe the two men were anything alike. But what if she were wrong?

The aroma of fried fish and hush puppies triggered her hunger as she walked into the fellowship hall. The weekly family night supper was in full swing. She hadn't eaten since the quick bite they'd had at the airport.

A familiar laugh drew her attention across the large room filled with people. Dix. He was standing beside Gwen Holman, his arm resting around her waist. They were speaking with an elderly couple, longtime members of the church.

The heat of humiliation sped upward through her veins. As she watched, Gwen smiled up at Dix and hugged him.

He hugged her back, his laughter rising above the chatter in the room.

Lena felt sick to her stomach. What a fool she was. What a silly, romantic, idiotic fool.

She turned and started for the exit, only to be stopped by the parents of one of her students. She ended the conversation as quickly and as politely as possible then started for the door again. Her stomach had stopped churning, but now her chest was compressed with anger.

"Lena. Wait. Where are you going? Aren't you going to stay and eat?"

The sound of Dix's voice knifed through her. She kept moving, but he took her arm and stopped her.

"Hey, what's up? You all right?"

Lena took a moment to calm down. She refused to make a scene here in the church in front of all these people. She had to get control of herself. She couldn't afford any more stupid mistakes where men were concerned. She pulled her arm from his grasp and looked him in the eyes. "Kelly tells me Mrs. Watson has made a donation to your cause."

"That's right."

"Is that how you finance your films? Other people's money?"

"Most movies are done that way. Yes."

"And what do they get in return? Free tickets? Or do they even get that much?"

Dix frowned, placing his hands on his hips. "What's this about, Lena?"

She shouldn't have opened up this can of worms, but she wasn't going to sit by and let members of her church family be hoodwinked by some slippery movie man.

"It's about me and how gullible I am." She turned and walked out of the building, praying Dix wouldn't follow but knowing he would.

"Lena. What are you talking about?"

"I'm talking about a slick-talking ladies' man who makes his living by charming other people out of their hard-earned money."

Dix reared back, holding up his hands. "Whoa. Slow down. What's going on?"

"First Mrs. Watson. Now Gwen Holman. It's obvious to me."

Dix's eyes darkened, and his jaw flexed rapidly.

"Well, it's not obvious to me. I think you owe me an explanation. And for the record, Mrs. Watson came to me. I didn't go to her. And Gwen has a friend who works at the Chamber of Commerce who deals with film shoots. A contact I happen to need."

Lena's anger deflated, leaving her feeling small. She didn't want to think badly of Dix. Maybe she was jumping to conclusions, shoving him into a Peter-sized cubbyhole. But the pain of Peter's betrayal wasn't something she'd ever get over, and she refused to be duped again. Past memories reinforced her indignation. "Always quick with an answer, aren't you?"

Dix crossed his arms over his chest. "When they're truthful, yes."

Lena turned away. "I've got to go." Disappointment and humiliation hovered over her shoulders as she walked briskly to the parking lot. She climbed into her car and shut the door, surprised that Dix had allowed her to drive off.

At home she changed clothes and sat down at the computer, searching out all she could find on Dix's film company, Parable Productions. She was deep into her research when a knock sounded on her back door.

She knew who it was. Dix. She debated whether to ignore him or to confront him and get it done with. No sense dragging this out. Reluctantly she walked into the kitchen, recognizing his broad frame through the window. She didn't want to talk to him, but in his defense, she'd found nothing questionable about his business.

"What do you want, Dix?" She called to him through the door, still hoping he might go and leave her alone.

"I want to talk, Lena. We can't leave things like this. You know that."

He was right, but her emotions were too confused right now. She wasn't sure she could think clearly. But she had a feeling he wouldn't go away until she let him in. She opened the door and stood aside for him to enter.

He looked tense, wound up, and ready to strike. Maybe a little defusing was in order. "Can I get you something to drink?" She saw the muscle in his jaw flex, then abruptly he relaxed.

"Sure. Fine." He took a seat at the kitchen table.

Lena fixed two glasses of iced tea and joined him at the table. He stared at her. She squirmed and searched for a place to start. "Why did Mrs. Watson give you money? Everyone knows she's as tightfisted as they come. She doesn't give money to anyone. She even tracks the money she gives to the church."

Dix leaned back in his chair, meeting her gaze directly. "You'll have to ask her. She called and asked if I could use the funds. I said yes. End of story. You want to tell me what this is all about?"

"Nothing. I happen to find it strange that you show up all charming and attentive to the congregation, and suddenly people are opening their wallets."

Dix set his jaw. A white line formed around his mouth. "I'm insulted by your assumptions, Lena. What have I done to make you so suspicious of me?" He studied her a moment. "Or did someone else lay the foundation of distrust?"

Lena looked away. Dix was too perceptive.

"Who was it? What did he do? Don't you think you owe me that? You've accused me of being a con artist out to bilk your church family."

"It wouldn't be the first time."

"It wouldn't happen on my watch." He leaned forward. "Lena, I thought we were friends. Why are you doing this? You owe me an explanation."

Shame and remorse bowed her head. He was right. She owed him an explanation. Especially for jumping to conclusions. She searched for a good place to start. "His name was Peter Cane. We met when I went back to college to get my masters degree. He came to our church with this mission to bring medical aid to children in Appalachia. The entire congregation got behind him. We held bake sales, rummage sales, donations poured in.

"I found myself helping him more and more, and soon we began to date and eventually got engaged. When it came time for him to leave to take the money to the mission field, he asked me to come with him."

"Did you?"

Lena scraped a fingernail over the back of her thumb. "I planned to. But then word came that there was no such ministry and that Peter had disappeared with the money. I was lucky I didn't go with him, but I couldn't face the church again. I found a new church home and concentrated all my energy on working and studying."

"And you thought I was like him? That I was here to bilk your church out of money with some moviemaking scam?"

Dix's genuine anger and hurt pierced her soul. "I'm sorry, but I had to be careful. I researched the studio on-line—"

"You dug into my company?" Dix stared at the ceiling a moment as if trying to rein in his anger. "Ask me anything, Lena. I'm an open book. My partner and I have nothing to hide. We're legit. We pay our taxes. We don't bilk little old ladies out of their life savings, and we don't steal beautiful women's hearts then break them."

Dix stood and turned his back. After a few moments she noticed his shoulders relax. Apparently he'd reached a decision. She knew she wasn't going to like it.

"Dix, I'm sorry. I know I shouldn't have jumped to conclusions, but—"

"No, you shouldn't have."

He turned and came toward her. His usually bright blue eyes were dark.

Her heart lodged in her throat. She fought to speak around it. "Dix…"

He stared at her a moment, then looked away. "I have work to do, Lena." He turned and walked out, letting the kitchen door slam loudly behind him.

The tears started the second he disappeared. Lena swiped the wetness from her cheeks. Her stomach tightened, forcing a sob into her throat. Oreo whimpered at her feet. Desperate for comfort, she scooped the little dog up into her arms and sought out the solace of her bedroom.

What had she done? She'd accused Dix of being a criminal. A man without scruples. Kelly was right about her. Somewhere she'd become suspicious and cynical, and she didn't like being this way.

Lena laid on the bed and rolled onto her side. Oreo snuggled up under her chin, licking her neck in an offer of concern. The real implications of her actions began to sink in, creating a knot in the center of her chest. Dix would never speak to her again. Ever. And she couldn't blame him. He'd been nothing but kind and funny and appreciative, and she'd repaid him with ugly distrust and suspiciousness.

Kindness.

One of the fruits of the Spirit. They'd been studying those qualities in her women's Bible study class. She'd shown no kindness to Dix. Nor any other Christian gesture. And because of her lingering wounds from Peter, she may have lost something important.

She stroked Oreo and took a closer look at herself. Something she realized she hadn't done in a good long while.

Peter's betrayal had left her with a broken heart. But God had healed it as He'd promised, and He'd opened her eyes to her susceptibility to charming men. She'd vowed to be careful and more vigilant in the future. But today she'd seen how deep her scars reached. She hadn't realized how much power Peter Cane still held over her.

Pulling Oreo into her arms, she closed her eyes. *God, help me see the truth. Set me free from the past.*

The morning air coming in through the windows was cool and damp. It had rained again last night. A quick, loud spring storm that had kept Lena tossing and turning for hours. She hadn't needed the thunder to keep her awake. Her own guilt and regret were enough.

The result was a throbbing headache and sore chest. All she wanted was a lot of coffee and a lot of quiet time. Oreo's claws clicked softly against the floor as he followed her to the kitchen. She stopped when a light tapping sounded at her back door. She looked up to see Dixon Edwards peering in through the door window.

"Hey." He waved.

She opened the door, unable to speak.

"Good morning."

She tensed, waiting for him to continue. She decided she'd follow his lead for the next move.

"That coffee smells good. Can you spare a cup?"

Lena relaxed inwardly. At least he wasn't going to yell at her. "Sure. Come on in."

He poured some for himself and doctored it with a little sugar. He turned and leaned against the counter, watching her over the rim of his cup. His penetrating blue eyes made her uneasy. "I'm sorry I got so angry last night, Lena. You caught me by surprise. Your accusations hurt."

She swallowed the lump in her throat. She was disappointed he didn't use her nickname. Then she'd know things were back to normal. "I'm sorry, too. I shouldn't have compared you to Peter."

"No. You shouldn't have. But I think I understand why you did."

She dared a glance at him and saw kindness in his eyes. "You do?"

He nodded, looking into his cup. "Yeah. I was sick awhile back. Cancer. My fiancée couldn't handle it, so she bailed."

The sadness in his eyes pierced her heart. He really did understand. "Oh Dix, I'm so sorry. How could she do that to you when you needed her most?"

Dix shrugged, a sardonic grin moving one corner of his mouth, releasing his deep dimple. "Better I discovered her true nature before the wedding than after the vows were taken."

"I know, but…" There was so much she wanted to say, to ask, but now didn't seem the proper time. "I guess we're both wounded in love and a little battle-scarred."

"Guess so. It tends to make you cynical if you're not careful."

Lena looked away. *Like me.*

"Just to set the record straight"—Dix placed his cup on the counter—"my partner and I don't need money for our productions. We look to legitimate investors for that. We

do, however, take donations for our foundation. It's called
Angel House, and it was set up to provide care for orphans
with special needs. That's what Mrs. Watson donated to,
Lena. To help kids."

Lena wished for a hole to disappear into. "I'm so sorry,
Dix."

He came toward her. "Let's put it behind us. I'd like to
be friends again if you're willing. We both reacted poorly.
I hope you'll forgive me."

"I'm the one who should be asking for your forgiveness. Will you?"

Dix took a long while to answer. "I still need your help.
Maybe we can put this behind us and concentrate on the
work. We're a good team, remember?"

Lena nodded.

"Good. Then I have a long list of places to locate today.
How soon can you be ready?"

Lena's spirits floated on air. "I'll meet you at the car
in ten minutes."

Dix smiled and winked. "Make it five."

*Thank You, God.* Her prayer had been answered. Dix
had forgiven her and wanted to continue their work together. She'd suspected for a while that there was more to
Dixon Edwards than she'd wanted to see. Her fears had
kept a nice pair of blinders over her eyes.

Today, she'd taken them off.


Dixon Edwards lowered himself into one of the deep-
cushioned chairs on the Arnez's patio and inhaled the
softly scented breeze of St. Augustine. The flowery,
slightly citrus scent made him think of Lena. He took a
swig of cola from his glass, wincing as it stung its way
down his throat. Dix grimaced. He needed to start drinking more water. Like Lena did.

He smiled as he thought about her. They'd had a good day together. Their initial awkwardness over last night's disagreement had passed quickly, and they'd resumed their easy friendship.

Lena had been almost flexible today. He'd thrown her a couple curves, changing his mind, changing directions, but she'd rolled with them all. He'd enjoyed every moment with her.

Too much so. And that could be a problem.

"Hey, Dix."

Rick Arnez patted him on the shoulder and joined him at the patio table. "How's it going?"

"Good. Productive."

"Lena proving to be helpful?"

"Yes. She had a hard time adjusting at first, but then she took to it like a pro."

Rick chuckled. "I'll bet. Lena can be a bit rigid, but once she puts her mind to something she's a bulldog." His friend studied him a moment. "Everything okay with you?"

"Sure. Why wouldn't they be?"

Rick shrugged. "You tell me. You've been acting a bit weird."

"Me? You're crazy."

"Maybe, but something is eating at you."

Dixon scraped his hair off his forehead. "I'm preoccupied, that's all. I'm out of my element with this location scouting. I want to make sure I cover all the bases. We don't have the budget for too many oversights."

Rick nodded. "I wasn't talking about your job. I was wondering about Lena."

"What about her?"

"I've seen you oblivious to women most men would kill to be with. You've resisted some of the most beautiful women like they were nothing but set dressing. But you're different with Lena. Is she getting to you?"

Dix shook his head. "No. She's a big help. She's good company, that's all."

"She's a very attractive woman. Or hadn't you noticed?"

For a moment, Dix wanted to punch his friend. But it wouldn't have solved anything. "I've noticed."

Rick was silent a long while before he spoke again. "Not every woman is like Mona."

Dix wished he'd punched him the first time.

He waited for the pain that usually accompanied hearing her name. All that surfaced this time was a small twinge of regret. "It's more than that, and you know it."

Rick crossed his arms over his chest. "Are you sure? Look, I know you want a wife, a family, something more than your job."

"Well, that's not going to happen. Besides, I'm fine. There's no room in my life for anything other than my ministry. You know that."

"I know that's what you tell yourself, but maybe you're not letting the Lord direct your future."

"Rick, this is my future. He gave me this passion. He opened the doors for me to have this ministry. I'm not going to be greedy and ask for more."

"So you think God has given you your share of blessings already, and He doesn't have any more?"

Dix rubbed his forehead. He'd forgotten how insightful his old friend could be. "No, but I've already got more than I deserve."

"Maybe you're settling for too little."

Rick's words replayed in Dix's mind as he tried to work later that night. He should never have come to St. Augustine. He could have let the regular scout come later and not worried about the lost time. But he'd wanted to see Rick, and he wanted to spend some time at the beach.

What he hadn't anticipated were the emotions that staying with Rick would unearth. Lena didn't help either. He was drawn to her in a way he'd never been to another woman, not even Mona.

His cancer diagnosis had shattered their relationship. She'd broken off the engagement, explaining her aversion to sick people. When she'd learned about the possible side effect of infertility, she'd recoiled in horror, refusing to discuss adoption or foster children. Her parting words still burned inside his heart. *"No normal woman wants to raise someone else's child. It's cruel of you to even think such a thing."*

Lena made him want to believe Mona was wrong. But how could he fault a woman for wanting the experience of giving birth? He wanted that, too. He'd always hoped for a son, a little guy to carry on the Edwards name. As his parents' only son, it was his responsibility. But it wasn't meant to be.

Dix shook off the somber thoughts and stared at the screen on his laptop. He needed to finish filling out the permit request to film at the Castillo. The first of many that would have to be filed before they could start shooting the picture next year. Trouble was, he couldn't concentrate. The only thing on his mind was Lena. And that was an impossible situation.

## Chapter 6

"So you'd rather get your hair cut than come play With me?"

Lena smiled into her phone. Dix sounded like a whiney little boy. "Yes. Your ego could benefit from a humility check."

"Ouch."

Dix could be really adorable when he chose. Since they'd made up, their time together had been thoroughly enjoyable. "So, do you think you can go scouting on your own this morning?"

A long beleaguered sigh came through the phone. "I suppose."

"Good. You need to get the beach scenes. You can either drive down to St. Augustine Beach—there are lots of small homes there—or you can go north and cross over to Vilano Beach. It's very quaint. St. Augustine Beach would probably be best."

"Okay, Sunshine. Will I see you later?"

"I'll call you when I'm done and meet you then."

Lena turned off her cell and smiled. Dixon Edwards was a very likable man. She especially liked his humorous bent. It was the one thing Peter had been lacking. She hadn't realized that until recently. Like Peter, Dix was a born charmer, but Dix's endearing qualities were always underscored with kindness and humor. Peter's charm had been affected, overdone, and he never really laughed. His humor always held a biting edge to it and was frequently condescending in tone. Effusive flattery had been his forte.

She should have noticed that sooner. Apparently her heart had been too busy creating fantasies to see the truth. She wanted to see the truth about Dix. But how could she trust her own judgment? How could she be sure this time?

She was still wondering when she walked into Sheila's Styles a short while later.

"What are we going to do today, Lena? A trim, or are you going to do something wild and crazy?"

Lena opened her mouth to speak and saw herself in the mirror. Her thick dark hair fell in its usual pageboy style, the one she'd worn for years. It was simple, easy to care for. No muss, no fuss.

Suddenly she wanted more. Different. "I think I'm ready for something more modern. What would you suggest?"

Sheila stared at her, gaping. "I don't believe it. You must have met a man."

Lena blushed. "Why do you say that?"

"Because you never do anything different, girlfriend. You are my most consistent customer."

Was she really that boring and predictable? "Am I?"

Sheila nodded. "Every time I ask you if you want a change you always say, 'This cut is very practical.'"

The hairdresser was right. That's what she said. "Well, I'm tired of practical."

Sheila chuckled. "Like I said, you must have met a man."

Lena gave her tresses over to the stylist, but each snip of the scissors filled her with regret. What was she thinking? What had come over her? Who knew what she'd look like when Sheila was done? She closed her eyes, mentally kicking herself for acting impulsively. She'd sworn never to do another impulsive thing ever, and yet here she sat, facing another disaster.

"Okay, open your eyes."

Lena's heart pounded. She was going to hate it. She knew she was. Too late now. Slowly, she opened her eyes and looked into the mirror. The reflection that greeted her was familiar but not. Soft fingers of dark hair brushed her forehead and cheeks. Her dark tresses ended below her chin, framing it with multiple layers.

"Well, what do you think?"

Lena smiled. She looked younger. Happier. The new softer, flowing hairstyle felt lighter, fresh. "I like it. Thank you, Sheila."

The woman shrugged. "I've been wanting to do that for a long time. You're too attractive to go around with a boring hairdo."

"It was more practical the other way."

Sheila pulled off the plastic drape and tossed it into the laundry bin. "Well, life is full of practical. What we all need is the special stuff. There's not nearly enough of that to go around."

Lena had to agree. Her new hairstyle made her feel special, and she liked it. She wondered if Dix would like it, too. After settling her bill, she walked out to her car, checking the time on her cell phone. He was probably still at the beach. She punched in his number, eager to hear his voice. "Hey, Dix."

"Are you all done?"

"I am. Where are you?"

"I'm down at St. Augustine Beach near a place called Beachcomber's. Can you join me?"

Her good mood faded a bit when he told her his location. She hadn't been there since she dated Peter. "Sure. I'll be there in a few minutes."

Closing her phone, she tried to ignore the knot of dread sitting in the pit of her stomach. Maybe she should call him back and tell him she had errands to run. But that would be cowardly. Besides, she wanted to see him. Maybe it was time to put the memories of Peter to rest, and maybe being on the beach with Dix was the perfect opportunity to do that.

But what if Dix only created new, painful memories? She needed to keep her guard up and not let masculine charm undermine her future.

Dix grinned and slid his cell into the back pocket of his jeans. Lena was on her way. He hadn't realized how much he valued her input until he didn't have it. He'd taken dozens of pictures, but the fun was missing.

Lena was always in his thoughts. He woke each morning anxious to see her, looking forward to the list of things they would do together. He wanted to be near her, to hear her voice, watch her expressions when he threw her a curve.

He stopped and inhaled a deep breath to clear his thoughts. He'd better back off before he lost his heart to the uptight teacher. Something about Lena made him feel vulnerable, as if she could see through his shield to the darkness deep inside.

If she looked too closely, if she shined her light too brightly, she would uncover his secret. She'd be so easy to love, but then he'd have to tell her the truth and break her heart. Lena deserved better.

The problem was, she'd planted a seed of hope in his heart when she said she didn't want a family of her own. He could understand her point of view. Raising her sisters, being their caretaker, had robbed her of a childhood and forced her to be a parent much too early.

Maybe Lena was the woman he'd been praying for. The one who could accept him the way he was.

A wave of shame washed over him, and he strolled toward the water's edge. *Father, forgive me. I'm content with the life You've given me. I'm committed to fulfilling Your plan for my life. I'll keep my eyes on the tasks of today and trust You for the blessings of tomorrow.*

Dix closed his eyes and waited for the peace that always touched him after he'd relinquished his problem to the Lord.

"Thank You, Father."

He glanced back at the road a short while later in time to see Lena drive up. He waved to her as she exited the car, and she waved back. His heart skipped a beat. He needed to get a grip on his emotions. Fast.

He started toward her across the beach, smiling as she tiptoed through the sand. She looked fresh in a simple green dress that lightly skimmed her curves. As she drew closer, he stopped, unsure of what he was seeing. Something about Lena was different, but he couldn't quite... Her hair. Her hair was different. It was softer around her face.

She drew near and he stared, pleasantly surprised at the change.

She looked at him expectantly. "Well?"

"You look fantastic. It makes you look—"

"Don't you dare say 'ten years younger.' "

He chuckled. "I was going to say you look brighter, carefree." He started to reach out and touch the soft tresses but thought better of it. He needed to keep boundaries. Better for both of them. "Well, now that you're here, Sunshine, want to go to work? I've only got a few more things to check out."

She glanced around the beach as if she were reluctant to stay.

"Something wrong?"

She hesitated a moment. "I haven't been to the beach in a while."

"Really? You haven't been to the beach and you live on the Florida coast?"

"Not every beach. Just this one."

She was withholding something. "Lena."

She crossed her arms over her chest. "I haven't been to this beach since Peter. Too many memories."

"Then let's make new ones."

She smiled that beautiful, dreamy smile, and he had to fight to keep from kissing her. He turned and jogged the few yards to where he'd left his backpack and pulled out the clipboard. "I can't do two things at once, Lena. Come give me a hand."

She walked toward him, applauding, an ornery smirk on her face.

"Funny." He handed her the clipboard. "Get to work, woman. We have more sites to scout out."

Lena walked at his side as he searched out the few remaining locations. One thought kept repeating in his mind—Lena belonged at his side.

Something he was beginning to want more and more.

A few hours later, they started back across the beach to their cars. Lena had been animated until the last few minutes. Dix mentally ran over their conversation, searching for a cause for her silence. He couldn't find anything. He sensed her introspection wasn't productive. Maybe some probing questions were in order. "Why don't you travel to the places you dream of, Lena? Why do you hold so tightly to your security?"

She was silent so long, Dix feared she wouldn't answer. "All I have is me. I have to take care of myself. I have to plan for the future. I have to be responsible."

"And you are, but that doesn't mean you can't take a vacation, or that you can't enjoy life and still be responsible."

She gave him a skeptical smirk. "Like you? Running around sightseeing, never in one place, always hopping from one city to the next, one country to the next."

"I don't do that all the time. Most of the time I'm in my office in Nashville working at my computer, or on the phone juggling five balls at a time trying to keep my company going."

"I can't just dash off someplace. What if something happened while I was away?"

"What if it did?"

Lena stared in disbelief. "I wouldn't be here to deal with it."

"So?"

"See, exactly my point. You have no idea what I'm talking about."

"Lena, do you believe in God?"

"You know I do."

"Do you believe He's in control, that He's sovereign?"

"Yes."

"But not over your day-to-day life. Only the big picture."

She raised her chin defensively. "He expects me to be a good steward."

"Agreed, but do you think He means for you to live so fearfully, so miserly?"

"I don't."

"You've created a little world where everything is under control. You have a nice little rut you follow and never veer from." He drew a line in the air. "You go from house to work and church. You live nice and safe inside your little furrow. You dream and you plan but never do. You hide in your safe, paid-for house in your soon-to-be-safe job. Why?"

"I'm practical."

"You're scared. You don't trust the Father to take care of you, to guide your future. Mostly you don't trust Him to provide for you in times of difficulty."

"He didn't before."

Dix stopped at her side. "What do you mean?"

Lena crossed her arms. "I prayed to God all the time when I was young to make my mother stop drinking. I asked God to give my dad a job with some stability, to make him care about us and take care of us, but He never did. God let me do it all. Instead of being a kid and playing with other kids, I was at home washing and cleaning and making sure my little sisters had food. That they went to school and church. Where was God then?"

Dix ached to hold her against his shoulder and ease her sadness. "Right beside you, Lena, giving you wisdom beyond your years so you could be there for your sisters."

Her jaw worked furiously, trying not to cry. "What about later, when I had to give up my college career to come back home and work to get my sisters through school? Where was His support then?"

"He found you a job. He made it possible for you to care for them."

"But there's never anyone to care about me." Lena turned away.

Dix heard the tears in her voice. He stepped close to her and held her shoulders in his hands, resting his cheek against the back of her head. "He cared about you. He always will."

"Then why didn't He send someone to help me, instead of leaving me all alone?"

"I'm sorry you had to go through that. I understand now why security is so important to you, but you already have that, Lena."

"How?"

"You told me you own your home. You have a steady job. With or without the promotion, a teacher can always find work. What more security can you expect?"

"I don't know, but I want to be prepared if anything should happen. That's not a bad thing."

"No one has that luxury, Lena. As a Christian you should know that. Life is unpredictable. Things happen. We don't always know what's best for us. So we have to trust that He does." Dix turned her around to face him. "That's why we have to depend on Him to bring us through."

Lena set her jaw. "I depended on my father, and look how that turned out. Never around when I needed him, only thinking of himself and never his children. He was a self-centered charmer who did what he wanted first, and whatever was left over, he gave to us."

Dix nodded and slipped his hands into his pockets. "Is that why you always refer to the Lord as God?"

"It's who He is."

"He's also our loving Father."

Lena shook her head.

"Is that how you think of God, as some distant, fearsome being who doesn't care about your struggles?"

"No, but..."

"Maybe you're confusing the actions of your father here with the actions of your Father in heaven. Don't limit God's love and grace in your life, Lena, because you're angry at Him."

"I know God loves me. I know He cares, but I'm alone, and I need to provide for my future. Everyone does."

"That's true to an extent, but God is in charge of your life. Trusting in your own wisdom and strength will always lead to failure and leave you with a life of fear and unhappiness."

Lena settled her purse on her shoulder and looked away. "It's not that simple."

She squared her shoulders, and Dix realized he'd gone too far. He'd put his foot in his mouth. When she turned and walked off toward her car, he was certain of it. It wasn't the first time he'd slipped into preacher mode. Not a good place for him. Definitely not a good place for him when he was dealing with Lena.

The phone was ringing when Lena unlocked her back door. The drive home from the beach was a blur, her thoughts consumed by things Dix had said. It was probably him calling, and she wasn't ready to talk to him.

A quick check of the screen revealed the call was from a business. One she didn't know. Relieved, she let it ring.

She changed her clothes, started a load of laundry, then pulled up her checking account and paid a few bills. A quick wipe-down of the kitchen put everything back in order. She retrieved the mail from the box and sorted through it. Her gaze scanned each return address, searching for the one that might contain the news she'd worked so hard for. It was too early to expect a reply about the job, but it didn't hurt to hope. Back in the kitchen she picked up Oreo and took his brush from the basket near his bed.

She carried the small dog to the lanai, sat on the lounge chair, and began to brush the tangles from Oreo's coat. She smiled, relishing the quiet moment with her pet. A sense of calm filtered over her mind. Everything was in its place and under control.

She stopped. Control.

She'd revealed part of herself to Dix today, a part she'd not realized herself until she'd spoken the words out loud. She was angry at God. She did hold Him responsible for her difficult childhood. He could have changed it, but He'd chosen not to.

Dix had tried to tell her she had no control over her life. He'd warned her not to trust her own strength to keep her life in order but to rely on God. But how did she do that? She'd spent her whole life balancing on a shaky fence. Never knowing when her life would be secure, or when it would be in upheaval. When her mother would be sober and behaving like a mother, or when she'd be passed out in the bedroom and it would be up to Lena to feed her sisters.

Later, there was the constant question of whether her father had worked enough to pay the bills to keep a roof over their head or if they'd have to eat cold cuts because the electricity was turned off. She never knew where her dad's paycheck went. She'd suspected he might be a closet gambler, though she'd never found proof. Probably his way of coping with his wife's alcoholism. The end result was she and her sisters had to pay the price for the failures of the adults in their lives.

Her thoughts pressed down on her chest, making it hard to breathe. She was so tired of being on guard against the surprises around the corner. She could never quite get everything in her life going in the same direction. If she could get control for just a moment, then…

Was Dix right? Was she depending upon her own strength instead of God's? Had her concept of God been distorted by her earthly father's failures? Was she striving for a sense of control that she could never achieve?

Oreo turned in her lap, his large dark eyes searching her face. She smiled and lifted one of his ears, gently brushing away the tangles. Holding the little dog always gave a sense of comfort.

Comfort.

Maybe that's what she'd been missing. She glanced at her Bible on the side table. She'd been so preoccupied with Dix, she hadn't opened it all week. Maybe she needed to reconnect. She placed Oreo beside her and opened the book to the current verse in her women's study class.

Fruits of the Spirit—love, joy, peace, patience, kindness, goodness, faithfulness, gentleness, self-control.

Her attention focused on two words: *joy* and *peace*. The two attributes she struggled with. No matter what she did, she could never be completely joyful or at peace.

Settling deeper into the chair, she began to read. There had to be an answer somewhere.

Lena laid her purse on the kitchen counter and turned to Dix, who nodded toward the fridge, seeking permission to get a bottle of cola. She nodded in return and hid a smile. He'd become very comfortable in her home over the last week. It was part of his personality, making himself at home wherever he went and making people feel at ease and relaxed.

Neither had mentioned the discussion from the beach yesterday. Instead, they'd spent the day out in Hastings. Dix had contacted the pastor he'd met earlier in the week and made arrangements to visit his church. It had been a lazy day. Dix had been more laid back than she'd seen him all week. He claimed they were hunting movie sites, but Lena had checked off only a small number of locations. They'd had a leisurely lunch at a local seafood restaurant and taken their time getting back to Anastasia Island.

Lena tried not to think about the week's end. Her obligation to Dix was nearly over. He hadn't mentioned any plans for tomorrow. She'd considered asking him to sit with her at church but hadn't found the right moment.

"Well, we're done with most of the legwork here in St. Augustine. Now it's time to do the paperwork." He took a swig of his drink. "Chasing down permits, talking to power companies, negotiating contracts with property owners."

"Sounds boring."

"It is. I'm glad I don't have to do this job all the time."

"How did you get into the producing business? I can't imagine there was an ad in the local paper saying, 'Christian producer wanted for new movie company.' "

Dix laughed and took a seat at her kitchen table. "No. Larry and I met when I was working in marketing. We attended the same church. When I realized what I wanted to do with my life, I called him. He had just formed his film company. I had some money to invest, and it fell together from there."

"Dix, I've been thinking about what you said…" The phone rang. Lena moved to the counter to pick it up, irritated at the interruption. The caller ID displayed the name Kelly. For a brief second she considered ignoring the call. "Hey, Kel, what's up?"

"I hate to bother you, but I really need you to come look at something over here."

"I'm kind of busy. Can I come later?"

"Please, I really need another opinion. Is Dix with you?"

Lena looked over at her companion. He was sitting at her table as if he belonged there. "Yes."

"Great." Kelly sighed in relief. "Bring him, too."

"All right. We'll be right there." Lena tried to hide her disappointment as she replaced the phone in its cradle. She had been looking forward to spending the evening with Dix. "Kelly needs us."

"Did she say why?"

"She has something she wants our help on."

Dix stood and held out his hand to her. She hesitated for a moment, warning herself to keep some reasonable emotional distance between herself and Dix. Another part of her wanted to take his hand and never let go.

She slipped her hand in his and allowed him to lead her out through the lanai and across the drive to Kelly's. She was puzzled when he walked toward the front door. "Why didn't you go to the back?"

"What? Oh, Rick's doing some renovations back there."

"I don't remember Kelly saying anything about renovations."

Dix pushed open the front door and waited for her to enter. She walked through the broad foyer and stepped into the living room.

"Surprise!"

The chorus of voices and laughter drove her back against Dix's chest. She was vaguely aware of his hands resting on her shoulders to steady her. She tried to grasp the situation. The familiar, smiling faces, the happy greetings. Balloons floating in clusters for decoration.

A surprise party for her birthday.

Her stomach heaved. Why would they do this to her? How could they plan a party without checking with her first? She forced a smile as her friends surged toward her.

She didn't want to hurt their feelings, but they all knew how she hated surprises.

The feel of Dix's solid form against her back gave her courage. "Oh wow. I never suspected a party." The smile on her face felt stiff.

"I knew you'd be surprised." Kelly pulled her away from Dix and into a warm hug, then she took Lena's arm, tugging her even farther away from Dix's comforting presence and into the center of the room. The coffee table was piled high with gifts.

Lena sat down on the sofa, trying to hide the shaking in her hands. Why had they done this? She glanced at Dix, who was studying her intently. His blue eyes narrowed. The noises in the room bombarded her. She was unable to distinguish words.

*Escape.*

She needed to escape and regroup. One of her fellow teachers bent down and hugged her. Lena used the moment afterward to stand, searching for an excuse to leave the chaos surrounding her. "I'm overwhelmed, y'all. I need a drink."

Kelly smiled and nodded. "Refreshments are in the dining room. Let's eat first, then we'll open presents."

While Rick was offering a blessing over the food, Lena slipped into the kitchen, trying to calm her nerves.

"Lena. What's going on?"

She winced at the sound of Dix's voice. Why couldn't everyone leave her alone and let her get control? Didn't they understand? "Nothing."

"Oh? You have a room full of friends wanting to celebrate your birthday, and you're hiding in the kitchen? I'd say something is definitely wrong."

Lena turned her back, searching for words to explain the way she felt. "They should have warned me."

"About a surprise party?" His tone was incredulous.

"I don't like surprises." She heard Dix moving toward her and quickly retreated by putting the kitchen island between them.

"Why not? This is a happy surprise, after all. It's not like you suddenly lost your job or got a call that your house burned down. It's a party from your friends."

"I like to know what's coming."

"Don't you think you're taking your control issue a little too far?"

Lena turned to face him. How dare he. "You don't know what you're talking about."

"Don't I? You're so afraid of being out of control that you can't even allow your closest friends to give you a party you don't know about."

"That's not it." He clearly had no idea what she was dealing with.

"Isn't it? You're worrying more about your own feelings than the spirit behind the gift your friends are giving you. You can't control every aspect of your life, Lena. If you think you can, you're lying to yourself. I suspect there's a lot of things you're lying to yourself about."

"It's not that I don't appreciate what they've done. It's just that—"

"You'd rather have control."

"You make it sound so selfish."

"In a way it is."

Lena set her jaw. "You have no right to say that."

"I'm your friend, and friends are truthful with each other even when it hurts."

"Does cruel count, too?"

Dix came toward her. "Lena. Have you ever stopped to consider your behavior from the other side? From your friends' point of view?"

"I don't know what you mean."

"They come together, out of love and affection for you, to give you a surprise party. Can you imagine their excitement and the fun they had doing this? Because they care about you. They want to show you how special you are to them."

"They could have invited me out to dinner."

Dix nodded and crossed his arms over his chest. "They could have. Then you would have had control, right? Maybe choosing the time, the restaurant?"

Lena shook her head. He was wrong. It wasn't about control, it was about… She couldn't explain even to herself.

"They chose a party. But instead of embracing their gift, you're here, hiding in the kitchen pouting because you didn't know about it in time to get control of yourself, your emotions, your schedule, your mind-set—"

"No."

"What kind of message do you think this is sending to your friends? You're telling them that their feelings for you aren't as important as your own sense of security. You're saying their opinion of you doesn't count unless it's filtered through you first."

"No, you're wrong." But even as she said the words she realized Dix was right. If she stood apart from her own feelings and looked at the situation from her friends' point of view, she appeared small and self-absorbed. That was far from the truth.

She was deeply moved by her friends' gesture, but she had no idea how to handle the situation because…she didn't know what was coming. Shame bowed her head. She loved each and every person here. She never intended to reject their gift or their affection.

Dix slipped an arm around her shoulders. "Lena, you've been so busy trying to control everything around you, trying to ward off anything unexpected, that you've shut yourself off from the Father's blessings."

Is that what she'd been doing? Was her fear and need for security blocking things that God wanted to give her?

"Lena? Where are you?"

Kelly's voice broke into her reflection. "In here." Her friend smiled mischievously when she saw the two of them sequestered in the kitchen.

"Oh. Sorry, you two. Didn't mean to intrude, but I have another surprise for Lena. Follow me."

Lena tensed. *Please, God, no more surprises.* Dix took her hand, and she remembered all the things he'd said. *God, give me peace to deal with this. I don't want to hurt my friends.* She held tightly to Dix's hand as they walked back into the living room. She stopped dead in her tracks when she saw her sister and niece in the middle of the room smiling and waving at her.

This was one surprise she could easily respond to. "Jeanie." She hurried to embrace her younger sister then turned to her niece. "Molly, this is such a wonderful surprise."

"I couldn't let your birthday pass unnoticed, and this seemed like more fun than a card in the mail."

Lena pulled her sister close, her anxiety easing in the familiar embrace. With Jeanie here, everything seemed manageable. She felt in control again. But for the first time in her life, she wondered if that sense of control was a good thing.

The evening passed quickly and pleasantly. Her friends didn't mention her initial reaction to the party, for which she was grateful. She was humbled by the depth of their affection.

"Are you ready to go?" Lena asked her sister as the party wound down. "You are staying at the house, aren't you? You aren't planning on driving back to Tampa tonight."

"Nope, not if you can handle the unexpected company. I know how you hate having your plans changed."

Lena winced. Apparently her obsession with control was obvious to everyone but her. "I'm thrilled."

Jeanie smiled. "I thought we'd go to church with you in the morning and then head back later in the afternoon."

"That's wonderful. I'm so glad to see you. We have so much to talk about."

Jeanie glanced over at Dix, who was talking with Rick. "I guess so."

"Oh, not about him. It's about a job I applied for. Vice principal at my school."

"Speaking of jobs." Jeanie rubbed her palms together. "I may be looking for one."

"Oh Jeanie, I'm sorry. What's happening?"

"I think Sea Change Designs is going under. The sluggish economy is killing us. No one can afford to redecorate their homes right now, and several of the planned resorts have been canceled. It makes it hard on designers like me. I don't suppose you'd be interested in remodeling the family home, would you?"

"What do you plan to do? If you lose the job, I mean."

Jeanie shrugged. "I might have to come home for a while. I don't want to, but I might have no choice."

"What about your house?"

"It's already on the market. I've seen these job cuts coming for a while."

"You're always welcome here, Jeanie. You know that. I'd love having you and Molly around."

"I know. I swore I'd never move back here. But I guess I could deal with it until I find a job. I'm worried that my next job might be across the country."

"Would that be a bad thing?"

"I've got to have work. I may not get a choice where it's located. But I love Florida. I'd rather not leave if I can help it."

Lena hugged her. "Then we'll start praying for something to turn up here in the Sunshine State."

Dix came to her side and touched her shoulder. "You ready to leave? I'll walk you home."

"Thank you, but Jeanie is staying with me. We're leaving right now." Jeanie glanced at Dix, and Lena had the impression something passed between them.

"I told Kelly I'd stay and help her clean up. Molly and I will be over shortly. You go ahead."

Dix muttered his good-byes and steered her toward the back door.

"What's your hurry?"

"I wanted to give you my gift in private, okay?"

Her heart warmed. She'd tried not to be disappointed when there had been no present from Dix in the pile. After all, they barely knew each other. "Present?"

"Did you think I'd forgotten?"

"I thought, well, you don't know me well, and…"

"Silly girl." He waited for her to open the back door then led her into the living room and guided her toward her computer. He turned on the monitor and waited.

She stared at the still-blank screen. "What am I supposed to see?"

"Patience."

The screen blinked to life, and a picture of her standing on the gun deck of the Castillo appeared. "Oh. I didn't know you took that picture." Before he could reply, another image appeared. Her standing beside the Old City gates. One by one the photos changed, each one showing her standing near landmarks, the beach, the lighthouse, the helicopter, the Bridge of Lions. Her heart warmed, and tears threatened.

"I thought it was time you had a screen saver showing you having real adventures."

His thoughtfulness touched her deeply. "Oh Dix, this is so sweet of you. I don't know what to say."

"Do you like it?"

"I love it. It's so much nicer to have real memories instead of fake ones."

"Isn't that what I've been trying to tell you all week?"

She looked at him over her shoulder. "Thank you, Dix. It's the perfect gift." The look in his eyes sent a shiver along her nerves. She wanted nothing more than to be in his arms.

He pulled her around to face him. It was as natural as breathing to step into his arms and rest her head against his chest. Her hands slid around his waist, and she inhaled his scent, making a detailed mental picture the way he'd taught her at the park that day.

Dix rested his chin on the top of her head. "Happy birthday, Sunshine."

Lena raised her head and looked into his clear blue eyes. His head tilted, and her heart responded with a fierce pounding in her chest. He was going to kiss her, and she had no control over it. None. What. So. Ever.

His lips were gentle at first, caressing and tender. The next kiss was more compelling. He held her close, and she sank into it, enjoying the nearness.

Slowly he pulled away, exhaling a soft sigh. "You go to my head, Sunshine. I'd better leave."

Lena clutched his arm, unwilling to see him leave but realizing the wisdom of his words. She looked into his eyes and smiled. "Thank you, Dix. For one of the most wonderful birthdays of my life."

He bent and kissed her forehead. "You're welcome, gentle Lena Clare."

Lena watched him walk to the back door, glancing over his shoulder and winking before he disappeared outside. She covered her face with her hands in happiness. She'd wondered what it would be like to kiss Dixon Edwards. Now she knew, and it exceeded all her expectations.

## Chapter 7

Lena closed her eyes, reliving the moment when she'd stepped into Dix's embrace. The tenderness in his kiss, and the hint of passion firmly held in check, consumed her thoughts. For one brief moment she allowed herself to dream about a different future. One she'd never thought possible. One in which someone took care of her instead of the other way around.

The creak of the back door jerked her out of her dream world. Jeanie entered the kitchen. "Well? How did it go? What did he get you? I want to know all the details."

Lena blushed and feigned ignorance. "Details about what?"

"Dix, of course. Kelly told me there was something brewing between you two, and it only took one glance to see she was right."

"I'm merely helping him out, that's all."

Jeanie crossed her arms over her chest. "Uh-huh. Sister

dear, he's adorable. And so sweet. You do know that this surprise party was all his idea, don't you?"

Lena stared at her younger sister. "What are you talking about? Kelly planned it, didn't she?"

Jeanie shook her head. "Nope." She came and stood in front of her. "Kelly mentioned your birthday was coming up, but the rest was Dix's idea. Kelly had to do the organization of course, and she mentioned inviting me and Molly, but no, it was all Dix's doing."

Lena shook her head, trying to process this new information. "Why would he do such a thing?"

Jeanie giggled. "Well, duh. I don't know. Maybe because he's falling in love with you."

"Don't be ridiculous." She frowned and faced her sister. "Where's Molly, by the way?"

"She's playing with Kelly's girls. She'll be here shortly. So what did he get you?"

Lena hugged her arms around her waist, feeling vulnerable and off balance. "A screen saver."

Jeanie frowned. "What? I thought it was going to be something romantic, like jewelry or a special trinket. Why a screen saver?"

Lena grinned and motioned her sister to join her in the living room corner office. She waited for her sister to react, giggling when Jeanie gasped in surprise.

"Oh Lena, this is too, too perfect. This man is a real treasure. You'd better hang on to him."

"He's not mine, sis."

Jeanie looked over at her with raised eyebrows. "Oh really? Well, he would be if you'd let go and claim him."

"Like a prize at a raffle?"

"Lena, I'm serious. The man adores you. You deserve someone like him. Someone fun, strong, and devoted. A good Christian man."

\* \* \*

Dixon walked slowly across Lena's lawn, his heart pounding violently in his chest. He stopped in the middle of Rick's driveway, lifting his eyes heavenward. What had he done? He should never have kissed Lena.

Laughter and muted conversation from Kelly's back door reached his ears. He didn't want to talk to anyone right now. Turning, he moved quickly toward the front lawn, finding refuge in the shadow of a giant oleander bush. The bench nearby was secluded and private. Any stray guests who might be leaving wouldn't see him here, even if the headlights of their cars flashed in his direction.

Dix bent forward, resting his forearms on his knees, head bowed. He'd kissed Lena. And in that moment knew he cared more for her than he'd ever intended. It went beyond simple attraction. Even admiration.

He turned his gaze to the water in the distance, searching his mind for answers. It had started as a fun game, a challenge, to see if he could get the prim little teacher to loosen up and embrace life more. But somewhere along the way he'd forgotten it was a game and allowed her to get under his skin. He'd let his guard down, and he might have to pay a very high, painful price for that mistake.

His own heart would be broken if he didn't get control of his emotions. Funny, he'd been pushing Lena to let go of her control, but he was the one now who had to exert self-control. Because if he didn't, Lena's heart would be broken again, and he couldn't let that happen. So how did he undo what he'd done? How did he take a relationship that had moved too quickly and slow it down and put it back on the path to simple friendship?

A car engine roared to life. Dix froze, not moving until the vehicle pulled out of the drive and onto the road.

He stood and made his way to the back door of Rick's

home. He'd have to play it nonchalant. As if the kiss was nothing more than a pleasant encounter. Nothing else.

The problem was, he was a lousy actor.

Lena thought about her sister's words as she crawled into bed. Dix was all the things Jeanie had said, but they'd only known each other a week. She couldn't deny the attraction was there. But a week wasn't long enough to develop genuine feelings between two people.

The kiss had rocked her to her toes, but the bliss of that moment was giving way to doubts and reservations in the quiet darkness of her room. The time had come to get her head out of the clouds and employ logic instead of emotion.

Lena rolled onto her side, staring at the moonlit shrubs outside her window. She was getting in over her head. She'd known from the moment she'd first met Dix that she needed to be careful. She vowed to keep her guard up, but she'd forgotten everything tonight in the midst of his thoughtful gift. She'd relinquished control for one brief moment, and her life had started to unravel. The result would be chaos.

She closed her eyes, attempting to sleep, but images of Dix and the kiss they'd shared refused to leave her thoughts. She sat up in bed and turned on the light. Maybe reading would help divert her focus. Reaching for her Bible and study book, she opened to the current lesson, smiling at the title of this week's topic.

Self control.

Exactly what she needed at the moment. Self-control where Dix was concerned. Another thought seeped into her mind. If she was so self-controlled, why didn't the peace and joy follow? Was she missing something?

* * *

Lena followed the restaurant hostess to the booth and slid in. Jeanie joined her in the opposite seat.

"This was a great idea. The *St. Augustine Record* listed the Oasis as the best breakfast in the city. Do you usually attend the early service? I thought you taught Sunday school."

Lena unwrapped her silverware and placed the napkin on her lap. "I have a friend filling in for me today. I wanted to spend extra time with you. We get together so rarely."

Jeanie nodded. "I know. I keep meaning to drive over, but Molly is into sports now, and there isn't enough time to do everything I like. Especially now, when I need to be looking for a new job."

Lena smiled and patted her sister's hand. "The road goes both ways between here and Tampa. I should try harder to stay in touch." She shook her head. "I can't believe how big Molly is. She's growing up so fast. I hope she wasn't too upset that we didn't invite her to eat with us."

Jeanie chuckled. "Not at all. She loves Kelly's girls. I'll have to pry her loose from them to get back home this afternoon."

The waitress handed them menus and took their drink order. Lena scanned the choices. It was a pointless gesture. She already knew what she wanted. Her favorite. Belgian waffle.

"So." Jeanie lowered her menu. "I didn't see Dixon Edwards at church this morning."

Lena tried to quell the rush of happiness that washed over her at the sound of his name. "He usually goes to the late service."

"Ah." Jeanie nodded, a knowing smirk on her lips.

Lena frowned. "What?" Her sister leaned toward her across the table.

"If I had to guess, I'd say you wanted to go to early church because you wanted to avoid seeing Dix. Right?"

"No, not right. I told you I wanted to spend the day with you. I wanted to get an early start, that's all." She wasn't about to admit that her sister was right. The kiss last night still had her reeling, and she needed more time to sort out her emotions before seeing him again.

"Did something happen last night that upset you? Did you have an argument?"

"No. We don't argue."

"You didn't like his gift? I thought it was so sweet and thoughtful. He really gave you something that— Wait. Did he kiss you?"

"Jeanie, that's none of your business." Lena focused all her attention on her drink. She did not want to get into this with her sister.

"He did, didn't he?" Jeanie leaned back in her seat. "Oh, I get it. And now you're all tied in knots wondering what the risks are if you allow yourself to care for him. Right?"

Lena squirmed inwardly when the barb struck home, but she wasn't about to admit it to her too-perceptive sibling. Thankfully the waitress returned to take their orders, and Lena took advantage of the opportunity to change the subject. "I ran into someone the other day who knew you."

Jeanie looked up. "Me? Who was it?"

"A helicopter pilot. His name was Zach something. Morrison. Montgomery. Do you remember him?"

Jeanie squared her shoulders and glanced downward, shaking her head. "No."

Apparently this was a subject her younger sister wanted to avoid, but turnabout was fair play. It wouldn't hurt Jeanie to be on the hot seat for a while. "He said you went to school together."

"We may have. I don't recall."

"He was a good-looking guy, Jeanie. Tall, well built. He had dark, wavy hair and gorgeous brown eyes. Oh, and he's a Christian to boot. Maybe you should look him up."

Lena's conscience smarted when she noticed her sister pleating her napkin. The lifelong habit spoke volumes about her stress levels. Lena wondered what had happened between her and this man that still bothered her years later.

Jeanie looked up and smiled. "I'd rather hear about this guy in your life."

Lena knew when she'd been trumped. If she hadn't been so inquisitive about Zach, maybe she wouldn't be caught explaining her relationship with Dix. "Dixon Edwards. Film mogul. Temporary location scout."

"Do you like him?"

"I do like him, but…" Lena toyed with her own napkin, gauging her words. "Something about him makes me uneasy."

"Can't be his looks."

"I'm serious. He's a charmer. He's always smiling, always friendly."

"And that's a bad thing?"

"It could be."

"Honestly, Lena. He seems like a nice guy. He was very attentive to you last night. Surely the man is serious sometimes. I mean, if he wasn't, he'd be a comedian, right?"

Lena thought about the morning she'd seen Dix on Kelly's deck. He'd appeared burdened, tormented. Several times she'd caught a glimpse of a sadness in his blue eyes. Perhaps his playfulness was merely a mask for some hidden pain. "No, he's not happy all the time."

"If you ask me, I think you're attracted, and you don't want to be, so you're looking for something wrong."

Lena wished she'd confided in her sister about Peter. Then she might understand her concerns. No one knew about him but a couple old friends she no longer saw. It had all happened so fast. Within six weeks she'd met Peter, fallen in love, and had her heart broken. She couldn't go through that again. "Maybe you're right, sis."

Jeanie reached over and squeezed her fingers. "Don't shut yourself off, sis. You need to stop being the big sister who's responsible for everything and do something special for yourself. It's time you stopped dreaming about traveling and do it."

There was that word again. Special. As if her sister had been a fly on the wall. Maybe she and Dix had some kind of plan to get her out of her rut. She sighed. Now she was calling it a rut. It was her life, and she was happy with it.

She was.

Lean smiled over at her sister. "I've only known him a week. You can't fall in love in seven days. Those kinds of relationships don't usually work."

"It worked for Tim and me. Until he died."

Lena's heart contracted. "Oh Jeanie, I'm so sorry. I didn't mean to bring that up."

"It's okay. It's been three years. I'm good. I only meant that there's no timetable on how long it takes to care about someone. It happens in its own way and its own time. Don't put boundaries and unnecessary limits on your feelings. This man could be part of your future."

Lena shook her head. "My future is in the administration of my school. That's all I ever wanted."

The waitress brought their order, and Lena turned her attention to the warm waffle. But a question kept repeating in her mind. Was her promotion really all she wanted? Or was there something more? Or someone?

Lena buttoned up her linen blouse then fastened a simple cross necklace around her neck. Glancing over her shoulder, she saw that she had only ten minutes to get Oreo's things together and leave. They were due at the home for their weekly visit.

She wished her niece could have stayed awhile longer so she could go with them. Molly had expressed a keen interest in learning about pet therapy. But Jeanie had to return to Tampa sooner than planned. She'd received an offer on her house, and she couldn't afford to miss the opportunity.

Grabbing up the bright blue collar and leash, Lena went in search of her Oreo. The back doorbell rang as she walked into the kitchen. Through the glass door she saw Dixon Edwards waiting. A smile came unbidden to her lips. Giddy happiness washed through her veins. She tried to appear calm and in control when she opened the door. Oh, how she'd missed him. "Good afternoon."

"I saw your sister leave, and I thought maybe you'd like to share some more birthday cake. Kelly sent the leftovers to you."

"Thanks. But I'm on my way out." She set the cake on the table. Her brief joy quickly turned to discomfort when she remembered their last encounter. She still hadn't sorted out her feelings about the kiss. "I have a therapy commitment."

Dix strolled into the kitchen and leaned against the counter. "You get counseling on the weekends?"

She couldn't help but laugh. One big point in his favor. He made her laugh. Peter never had. "No. Pet therapy. Oreo and I have a standing arrangement with the White Beach Home on Sunday afternoons."

Dix straightened and smiled. "Can I come? I have to admit I'm puzzled by this whole therapy idea."

She wasn't sure she wanted to be that close to Dix yet. Memories of last night still lingered in her mind, but he looked so excited. Like a little boy off on a new adventure. "If you'd like, but I'm leaving in a few minutes."

Dix spread his arms and flashed a dimple. "I'm ready if you are. How did you get involved with this dog therapy thing in the first place?"

Lena buckled the collar around Oreo's neck and placed him inside the small carrier. "My neighbor. She lived where Kelly's house is now. It was a little bungalow then. Rick and Kelly tore it down and built the modern house they have now. Mrs. Russell had been our neighbor as long as I could remember. She became ill, and when I'd go to visit her, I'd take our dog Pixie. Having the dog in her lap and petting it always calmed her.

"I met Josh years later when I started teaching. He's a vet. We went to the same school, but he was my baby sister Suzanna's age. He'd started a therapy pets program and suggested that Oreo would be a good candidate, so I joined up. Oreo's an old pro now."

Dix followed her to the car. After securing the kennel, they headed out to the home.

"So what exactly does petting an animal have to do with the elderly?"

"Oh, it's not only them. Everyone can benefit from the love of a pet. Abused kids respond extremely well. Oftentimes they'll open up after spending time with an animal. Oreo and I have visited mental health centers, prisons, juvenile halls—anywhere people are hurting. Petting animals increases a person's will to live. They may not feel comfortable hugging another human being, but they'll not hesitate to love on a dog or a cat. I tend to focus on the elderly because that's where Oreo fits best."

"Do you have to have special training?"

"Some. But there's not much for Oreo beyond basic

obedience skills. It's mainly a matter of the dog having a gentle nature."

"So these dogs are different from seeing-eye dogs."

"Completely. Those are service animals. They're trained from birth to assist the handicapped."

Lena waited for the light to change then steered the car around the corner toward the home.

"Are all the dogs small like yours?"

Lena chuckled. "No. They can be big, small, rescued, or pedigreed. Cats and dogs are mainly used, but in some situations horses and ponies are helpful. Josh, the founder of the Pet Partners organization, has a Dalmatian he takes to visit kids. They love him. They've all seen the *101 Dalmatians* movie, and they love being able to interact with Noley."

Lena pulled the car to a stop near the front door of the sprawling senior home. "Are you ready for a new adventure?"

Dix grinned, his eyes twinkling. "I never thought I'd hear you say that to me. Let's rock and roll."

Dix followed Lena up the walkway, carrying the small kennel that held Oreo. His admiration for Lena Butler had doubled on the ride over. He'd never met anyone with such a huge heart. He couldn't help but wonder if there was room in that sweet heart for someone like him.

Once inside, they checked in and went to room eighty-six. An elderly woman answered. Her excitement at seeing Lena and Oreo touched his heart.

"Oh, come in. Come in. I'm so happy to see you." The woman bent down and peered into the kennel. "There's my little sweetie."

Lena unfastened the cage and let Oreo out. The animal went immediately to the woman, his tail flying like a flag in a storm.

"Mrs. Ella, this is Dixon Edwards. A friend of mine. Dix, this is Ella Beltran."

"Good to meet you."

Ella waved them to be seated then retreated to her recliner and sat down. Oreo waited anxiously at her feet. When she patted her lap, the dog leaped up and sat, its big eyes never leaving the older woman's face.

"Oh, it's so good to see you. Such a handsome boy, aren't you?"

Dix waited for Lena to pick up the conversation, but she remained silent. He caught her gaze and raised an eyebrow.

She leaned close and whispered. "Ella likes to have one-on-one time with Oreo. We'll pretend we're not here unless she wants to talk."

The older woman spoke softly to Oreo, stroking his back and scratching the top of his head. She picked up a brush from the side table and began brushing the black-and-white coat.

After a half an hour, Ella looked over at Lena and smiled. "Thank you for bringing him. He's such a sweet thing."

Lena stood and collected her pet. "You're welcome. We'll see you next week."

Lena kept Oreo on the leash as she headed for the door, so Dix picked up the carrier. After saying their good-byes, he followed Lena down the corridor. "That was amazing. I could see her relaxing as she spent time with the dog."

Lena turned and smiled up at him. "I know. I love doing this. Maybe now you can understand why it's so important to keep Josh's organization going."

Lena stopped in the large community room they'd passed on the way in. "Good afternoon, everyone. Oreo and I have come to visit with you. Would anyone like to hold or pet my little dog?"

Several people came forward, all chattering at once. Lena was in her element, so Dix found a spot near the wall where he could observe the interactions. Most everyone in the room took a turn playing with the dog. A few refused. One man in a wheelchair scowled the entire time, as if disapproving of the situation. Dix held his breath when the man shouted at Lena.

"Hey. Bring that useless thing over here, and let me get a look at it."

Lena smiled and gave Oreo the command to heel as she approached the man. "This is Oreo. He's a Shih Tzu breed."

"Don't you have any real dogs?"

Lena nodded. "We do. I can have someone bring a shepherd or a lab to visit if you'd like."

The man's scowl deepened. All Dix's protective instincts kicked in. He would not let this old man bully Lena.

"Put that critter up here. Let me take a look at it."

Lena placed the small dog in his lap and stood back. Dix held his breath, not knowing what to expect. To his shock, the man began to stroke the little dog. He muttered something under his breath that caused Lena to stifle a grin. Dix made a mental note to ask her about it on the way home.

It was over an hour later when they placed the kennel in the backseat and started for home. Nearly every one of the residents had taken a turn playing with Oreo.

"You have an amazing ministry." He glanced over at Lena, who flashed him a pleased smile.

"I love it. It's so gratifying to see these people relax and connect with Oreo."

"What did the old guy say? I couldn't hear him."

Lena laughed and shook her head. "He said the stupid dog's hair was too long."

Dix frowned. "That seems rude."

"No, you don't understand. I've been coming to this home for nearly a year, and Mr. Kern has never even looked at Oreo. He's been the voice of doom from day one. Today was a major breakthrough. I'm thrilled."

Once back at Lena's, Dix realized he didn't want the day to end. "How about some dinner? We could find a quiet place. Somewhere on the water, maybe?"

"That sounds nice, but..." Lena fingered the place mat on the table. "I've got to go back to work tomorrow, and there's a lot I need to do. I've let so much go because of helping you out, and now I've got to play catch-up."

Dix tried to hide his disappointment. "Sure. I understand." He started toward the door. "I'm going to be around for a few more weeks, remember. I could still use your help. You're the best guide I've ever had."

Lena smiled. "Thanks. I'd be happy to help any way I can."

Dix gestured toward Rick and Kelly's house. "I'm right next door."

"I know."

"Don't be a stranger."

Lena's smile faded. "You either."

Dix's spirits rose. She still wanted to see him. "Not a chance, Sunshine." He waved and strode out the door, his hopes riding a rising tide. *Thank You, Lord. You are awesome.*

Lena exhaled the breath she'd been holding from the moment Dix had asked her to dinner. She wanted desperately to say yes. But her sense of responsibility had risen up to confront her. It had been an exciting, surprising week, and she'd enjoyed every moment, but it was time to put an end to her tour guide role and get back to her real life.

Her attraction for Dix was out of hand. Going back to her job would help put it all into perspective. This past week was nothing more than a short romantic interlude, a brief encounter with a charming man that meant nothing.

Lena glanced down at the kitchen table and the birthday cake Kelly had sent over. She needed to go and thank her for everything. But not in person. Dix was there, and she didn't want to run into him again.

After changing into comfy loungewear, Lena went in search of her portable phone. The one she could never keep track of. Mid-search, the phone rang from the back bedroom. Quickly she retrieved it. Kelly was calling. She punched the Talk button. "Hey, I was getting ready to call you and thank you for the party and the cake."

"Well, you know it was all Dix's idea."

"I know. Jeanie told me. It was very sweet of him."

"That's because he's sweet on you."

"You sound like my sister. We've only known each other a week. Only friends."

"Rick and I knew from the first moment we met."

Lena rubbed her forehead. She didn't want to hear any more testimonials about love at first sight. It was absurd. She knew firsthand what a disaster it could turn out to be. She quickly said her good-byes then sat down at the computer, only to feel the sting of tears when the screen saver dissolved into a picture of her at the Castillo. She tapped the touch pad quickly making the image disappear.

For the first time in years, she wished she didn't have to go back to work.

## Chapter 8

Lena dropped her keys on the kitchen counter and sighed. It had been a very long Monday. The children had been hard to control. They were still wound up from their week off.

Part of the fault might have been hers. She'd found it hard to concentrate herself. It was something she'd never experienced before. Once she was inside her classroom, her focus was on the students. It was all about them. Teaching, listening, opening new avenues of learning. Making sure the children had all the attention they needed.

But today she'd been distracted with thoughts of Dixon Edwards. She'd hoped going back to work, resuming her normal, predictable routine, would be a welcome and satisfying event. Dix had kept her off balance and on the go the entire week.

So why was she so antsy today? She'd checked her phone several times, wondering if he'd called. She caught herself wanting to call him and remind him of the sites he still had to locate and the appointment he had with the Chamber of Commerce representative. Then there was the deadline for the permits that had to be filed and the locations she'd thought of that might work for a scene.

She didn't know what was wrong with her. She never got off track at work.

Walking into her bedroom, she kicked off her shoes then changed into cotton lounge pants and a T-shirt with a picture of the Bridge of Lions on the front. After taking out her contacts, she put on her glasses and looked at her reflection in the bathroom mirror. Dix had said he liked her in glasses. Silly man. Everyone knew men didn't make passes at girls who wore glasses.

But he had.

And she'd wanted him to.

Lena shook her head, walked back into the kitchen, and let Oreo out the back door. She had to rein in her growing attraction to Dix Edwards. But the fact was, she'd missed him today. And to her shock, she missed the excitement and unpredictability he'd brought to her life.

Picking up her smartphone, she checked for missed calls. Nothing appeared on the screen. No messages were left on her answering machine either. Her gaze drifted to the kitchen table. She could see Dix sitting there, discussing his business, looking as if he belonged in her home. She'd never be able to come into this room without thinking of him.

Sighing, she fixed a glass of tea, returned to the living room, and curled up on the sofa, drawing the afghan over her legs. Something about the room felt different. The sense of comfort and security were missing. She scanned the room, taking a mental inventory of her home. Everything was in its place. Everything was as it should be. But the house seemed empty. Home had always been her sanctuary. Her haven.

Tonight it merely felt lonely.

Everywhere she looked triggered memories of Dix—leaning against the archway to her living room, teasing her about her messy computer desk, standing in the middle of this room and pulling her into his arms.

Lena bit her lip. He'd only been inside her home a few times during the last week, but he'd left an indelible impression.

She needed a distraction. Spying the movie that had come in the mail last week, she rose and placed it in the DVD player. But as she waited for the movie to load, the screen saver on her computer monitor drew her attention. With each revolving image her smile grew, and sweet memories embraced her. She rose and shut off the monitor.

But turning off the computer screen didn't stop the memories inside her head. Dix had ruined everything. He'd changed the feel in her home. He'd made her restless and made her question her life choices.

He'd accused her of hiding, of using her house as a place to insulate herself from life and maintain control. She didn't want to believe he was right, but as she thought about her daily life she began to see she only ventured out to places she was sure of, confident she could control her environment.

Oreo snuggled against her legs. She scratched his ears. How was it possible that he knew more about her than she did herself? "What is it about these charming men that I'm so drawn to? Huh, Oreo?" The dog looked up at her curiously. Peter had been a smooth talker. A smiling, silver-tongued, handsome scoundrel. A man who took other people's money and faith and absconded with them.

Lena rubbed her forehead. She didn't honestly believe

Dix was like Peter. He was exactly as he appeared—a man who loved his work. Friendly, outgoing, a people person.

And she missed him. For the first time in a long time, she wasn't content to hide inside her home. She wanted to be out with Dix. How could he have had such a profound effect on her in such a short time?

She needed to get a grip. He'd be gone in a few more weeks, and she had her dream of security within reach. The decision about the vice principal's job was due by the end of the month, and she'd heard from a friend that she was the front-runner for the position. The timing was perfect. Dix would go his way, she would go hers. She to her secure future. He, off to another adventure.

Lena glanced at the slick photo book on her coffee table with Heidelberg Castle on the cover. If she got the job, she'd made herself a promise to take her first vacation to Germany. Maybe she'd see if her sister Suzanna could go with her. Traveling was no fun alone.

Her gaze drifted to her cell phone sitting silently on the end table next to her. She could call him. See how he was doing. She reached for the phone then pulled back. She had no legitimate reason to call Dix. Only her own curiosity and longing to see him.

Pulling Oreo into her arms, she buried her face in the soft, warm fur. "I miss him." Maybe she was over-thinking the whole thing. It was only a friendly phone call, after all.

She reached for the phone again and jumped when the ringtone suddenly blared. The ID made her smile and her heart beat triple time. "Hello, Dix."

"Hello, Lena. How was your first day back at the salt mines?"

"My classroom isn't a salt mine."

Dix chuckled. "Twenty-five first graders? Oh, that definitely qualifies as a hard hat kind of job."

"My day was fine. How about yours?"

"Productive. I've filed the commercial use authorizations with the National Park Service, and my contact at the Chamber is experienced with film-shoot requirements. She's a godsend."

Lena's heart chilled. "She?"

"Yeah, her name is Tiffany, and she is incredible."

"So you'll be working with her all the time now?"

"Yes. She'll make things easier. Thankfully Tina, the regular location scout, has been in touch with the Florida Film Commission, so my job is still the grunt work. Tracking down locations."

Disappointment clogged her throat. Dix would be touring with Tiffany now. He wouldn't even need her to help with that any longer. There was a silence on the connection, and Lena searched for something else to say. Dix beat her to it.

"Are you jealous?"

Heat rushed into her face. She was glad Dix couldn't see her. "No. What a ridiculous idea."

"Sure?"

Her heart fluttered at the teasing tone in Dix's voice. "Positive."

"Good. No need to be. I still need your help, you know."

"Doing what?"

"Keeping me company."

"When? I'm at work all day, and you'll be…busy."

"Ah Sunshine. I'll never be too busy for you. In fact, can I come over now? I won't stay long. I've missed you."

Lena knew she should say *no*, but the word *yes* came out of her mouth.

"I'll be right over."

He was knocking at the door before she could rise from

the sofa. She met him at the kitchen door. "Were you standing there when you called?"

Dix grinned sheepishly and pointed to the lanai door. She laughed and let him in.

He took her shoulders in his hands and kissed her forehead. "Don't suppose you could play hooky tomorrow?"

"No more than you can."

Dix smiled and took her hand. "We'd better sit outside. I don't trust myself around you. You're way too adorable."

They settled on the swing, and Dix listened intently as she described her day. Before she knew it, Dix rose to leave.

"It's late. I'd better go."

"Okay. Will I see you tomorrow?"

"Of course." He bent and placed a quick kiss on her lips, then turned and walked out the door.

Lena scooped up Oreo and headed to bed. Something told her she'd have pleasant dreams tonight.


Lena took one last look at her classroom, making sure everything was in place for tomorrow. The children had been better today, finally readjusting to the daily routine. She'd been more focused herself. But she still missed being with Dix. They'd spent over an hour last night talking about places he'd been and places she dreamed of going. It would be wonderful to have someone to share her day with, someone who understood.

Lena collected her belongings, turned out the lights in her classroom, and started down the corridor. She loved teaching. She loved being in the school. She loved everything about it.

Pressing the push bar on the exterior door, she walked out of the building, exchanging a few words with her colleagues as they passed. If she got the vice principal job, she'd miss the interaction with the children and the other teachers. But the trade-off, her future security, would make up for it.

Walking around the corner of the building, she glanced at her car and froze. A man was leaning against it, his arms resting in his pockets, feet crossed at the ankles.

Dix.

A pale green polo shirt stretched across his broad shoulders. Khaki cargo shorts exposed well muscled calves. Boat shoes finished off the outfit. He looked good, but she missed the jeans and T-shirt style he'd sported last week.

She couldn't keep the smile from her face when she drew near him. "You've gone all native on me." She glanced downward. "Nice legs."

Dix grinned back at her. "It's hot down here."

"I know. What are you doing here?"

He smiled. "I'm stranded."

"What?"

"Yep. Tiffany dumped me here and told me to find my own way home."

Lena peered at him over her sunglasses. "Did you insult her?"

"No." He pushed away from the car and took her satchel from her. "I asked her to leave me here. I was hoping you would take pity on me and let me go home with you."

"What am I supposed to do with you?"

Dix smiled and opened her door. "Feed me?"

"I thought you were supposed to take care of expenses for this scouting trip."

"We're not scouting."

"Right."

Lena started the engine and eased out of the parking lot and onto the highway. Her heart pounded so violently she wondered if he could hear it. "Why are you really here, Dix?"

Dix studied her a moment, bringing a warm flush to her cheeks. "I missed you."

Her heart skipped a beat. "I doubt that."

He reached over and touched her hand. "Don't."

She wasn't sure what to make of his comment. She knew what she wanted to believe. She focused her attention on the road ahead. "How did it go today?"

Dix stretched his legs and leaned further back in the passenger seat. "Great. Looks like the majority of my locations will work on all levels. Plenty of room for vehicles. Power is good. Flight patterns overhead aren't a problem either. I even learned the local 'connections' aren't an issue."

"What do you mean?"

Dix pushed his nose to one side and bobbed his eyebrows up and down.

"The mob. Are you serious?"

"As a heart attack."

Lena struggled to digest that information. "Scouting locations sounds like such a simple thing."

"No job is as easy as it appears."

Lena pulled into the driveway and into the carport.

Dix came around to the driver's side and met her as she got out. He placed one arm on the roof, pinning her between him and the car. "So, you want to get a bite to eat?"

It would be so easy to say yes. She wanted to say yes. But she needed space. Too much had happened too quickly. "Maybe later. I have some things to do this afternoon."

Dix reached over and fingered a strand of her hair, sending her heart into quick time. "Your to-do list?"

"I can't scout all the time." She eased away from him.

"I really do need time to get caught up on things around the house."

"Okay. I'll give you a bye this time. Maybe we can order pizza later."

Lena avoided his gaze. "I don't know, Dix. I..." She felt him straighten beside her.

"Sure. I understand." He glanced across the street. "I think I'll go check out your pier. I'll call you later."

"Okay." Lena watched him walk away, a veil of sadness and regret settling over her heart. Something about his stride caught her attention. Something odd. The buoyancy was gone. His shoulders were slightly slumped, his hands shoved into his pockets. His attitude was reminiscent of the morning she'd seen him on Kelly's deck looking so somber and dejected.

He walked across the street and made his way along the wooden walkway. She couldn't shake the thought that Dix looked lonely. Even lost. If she didn't know better, she'd say that was impossible. But she'd seen a few of his dark moments. Everyone had them. Even happy-go-lucky types like Dix.

What if he'd invited her along because he didn't want to be alone? What if he needed a friend right now? Going to the pier filled her with dread, but maybe it was time to put that memory to rest along with the others she'd buried this past week.

Quickly she deposited her satchel and purse in the house then hurried down the driveway. Dix was standing midway along the boardwalk, staring out at the water. She slowed her pace, heart pounding as she neared the first wooden board. She kept her mind focused on Dix and not the memories of the other man she'd met on this pier. Her heeled sandals clicked loudly on each board as she walked.

Dix turned as she approached, a deep frown on his face.

She stopped in her tracks, regretting her impulse to join him. He looked angry, dark, and fierce. Nothing at all like the carefree man she'd come to know.

Who was this other man, and what dark demons plagued him? She waited for him to speak to tell her to go away.

The sadness in his eyes lifted a bit. "Hello, Lena. Change your mind?"

"I thought you might need some company."

A small smile moved one corner of his mouth. "I'd like that." He held out his hand to her.

She was reluctant to take it, to touch him, but the sadness in his eyes wouldn't let her refuse. She wanted to help. She took his hand, and the warmth in his touch sent tingles along every nerve.

He turned and started walking toward the end of the pier where it widened into a covered seating area. She walked quietly by his side, waiting for him to speak.

"Why don't you come out here anymore?"

His words caught her off guard. She started to repeat her usual excuse but realized she'd already confided a good deal to him. No reason to keep anything else hidden. "This is where Peter told me he loved me. We spent the day touring the city. It was the only time I'd managed to get him to leave Tampa and come visit my hometown."

Dix studied her a long moment. "Do you like being out here, surrounded by the water?"

Another question she hadn't anticipated. She had to think for a moment. She did miss coming out here. She hadn't realized how much until she stepped onto the first wooden plank a few moments ago. "Yes."

"So you let that bad memory of him steal your joy? You allowed him to keep you from the beach and from the pier in front of your home. What else are you letting him steal from you, Sunshine?"

"It's not like that."

"What is it like, Lena? Why have you given this jerk power over your life? It's not like you didn't see what kind of man he was and dump him."

The blood drained from her face, and she pulled her hand from his grasp, turning away to stare at the water. He'd caught her in her lie. No reason to hide it any longer. She kept her eyes averted. She didn't want to see his disappointment in her when she told him the truth. "I didn't tell you the whole truth about Peter."

"What do you mean?"

Her hands grew damp, and she clasped and unclasped her fingers while she searched for the words. "I didn't change my mind about Peter. He changed it for me."

Dix moved up beside her, resting his forearms on the railing and lacing his fingers. "I don't understand."

Lena closed her eyes, asking God for strength. "He said he'd received a message from a church in Pennsylvania that wanted to make a large donation to his cause. He felt he should accept it in person. He was going to make all the travel arrangements, and I was to meet him the next morning."

"But you didn't go."

She shook her head. "I went. When I got to the hotel, there was a note from him saying he wasn't coming."

"Did he say why?"

The tightness in her throat made it hard to speak. She nodded and struggled to clear her throat. Now that she'd come this far, she might as well confess the whole pitiful tale.

"He wasn't coming because he'd gotten married. Apparently I was merely a useful tool in his scheme. Once he'd completed his scam he went back to the woman he really loved."

Lena wrapped her arms around her waist. "How could I have been so blind and gullible? I believed he loved me."

"Oh Lena."

Dix straightened beside her. She held her breath, praying he wouldn't touch her. Because if he did, she would shatter into a thousand pieces.

"So you told everyone you called it off to save face." There was no condescension in his tone, only quiet understanding. "I did something similar when Mona left me."

"You did?" She glanced over at him to see if he was serious.

Dix nodded. "I told my family and friends we'd broken up before my diagnosis and that I hadn't gotten around to telling them. Pride makes us do strange things, huh?"

Lena nodded. "I've never told anyone the truth. Not even my sisters. I'm not sure why I told you."

"Maybe because you thought I'd understand. Or maybe because you were finally ready to confront the fear and pain."

"Maybe."

"What happened then?"

"I didn't have much choice but to come home. I'd given up everything to go with him. I quit my job, dropped out of school, and gave him all the money I had. I vowed that day to never do anything impulsive again."

"Is that when you shut your heart away, too?"

"I haven't."

"Come on, Lena, you've closed yourself off from God and from life because you're afraid of having your heart broken again. You've decided that doing anything impulsive or spontaneous equates to disaster."

"That's not true. God is a big part of my life. I have plenty of things I enjoy. Just because I don't run all over the globe doesn't mean I'm closed off."

Dix shifted his frame, leaning his hip against the railing, forcing her to look at him. "Maybe not all of you, but you have little strongholds that are keeping you locked up."

There was some truth to what he said. "Can you blame me?"

"Maybe not. I only want you to adjust your point of view a little. Life is all about how you perceive things. Me, I see everything new and unexpected as an adventure, a possibility. And you see them as obstacles, something dangerous and risky."

Dix laid his hand over hers where it rested on the wooden rail. "I understand your fear of letting go of things that are safe and secure. But you're too special to hide yourself away in that house. You've got so much love and joy to share." Dix stopped. "I'm sorry. I shouldn't be lecturing you when I'm the one that needs a kick in the pants."

Dix turned away, staring out at the water. Lena's concern grew. As much as she hated to admit it, she missed his happy-go-lucky side. "What's wrong? I've never seen you so serious."

"Nothing I can change."

He took her hand and started back down the boardwalk at a slow pace. The afternoon breeze danced around them, heavy with the salty sea air. The gently lapping water splashed softly against the pylons.

"Something is bothering you. What happened to the fun guy I met last week?"

A muscle in Dix's jaw flexed. "Yeah. Good old Dix. Never at a loss for words, always a laugh a minute." His thumb rubbed her hand slowly. "I have to be that way to get my job done. But I'm not always like that. Sometimes being charming isn't as easy as it looks."

She understood what he meant. There were times when she had to force herself to be social. "I know. I'm not that comfortable around people. I'd rather be in my home, but I know if I'm not careful I could end up a hermit. I think that was one of the reasons I fell for Peter. I liked his easy way with people. He was everything I wasn't. I never bothered to look any deeper. Maybe if I had, I would have seen he was empty and shallow."

"Bingo." Dix chuckled softly. "Mona was a head-turner. A woman no man could resist. And she picked me. I never thought beyond the way she made me feel in the moment."

"We're a sorry pair, aren't we?"

Dix stopped and faced her. "Or a very fortunate pair. Maybe we should look at our situations as blessings. The Father prevented us from marrying the wrong people. I know Mona wasn't the right woman for me. And from what you've told me, if you'd married Peter you'd have ended up with the same kind of man your father was."

Lena looked into his eyes. She'd never considered that aspect of her relationship with Peter. A part of her was grateful that she'd learned his true nature before marrying him. The other part of her could never understand how an intelligent woman like herself could have been so blind. She couldn't make the same mistake again. "But will we know when we meet the right people?"

"I'm praying I will."

Dix reached out and drew her into his arms, resting his chin on the top of her head. She closed her eyes, reveling in his embrace.

"Gentle Lena Clare, what are you doing to me?"

"What do you mean?" She pulled out of his embrace, her hands resting at his waist, and looked up at into blue eyes that matched the sky above them.

"I thought I had everything I needed. I thanked the Father every day for my ministry, my singled-minded devotion to spreading His light to the best of my ability. A one-man crusade to bring Christian film to the masses."

"What's changed?"

He stroked her hair, fingering the fine strands. "I met you. My ministry isn't enough anymore, Lena."

"Oh Dix. Please don't tell me you're thinking of quitting."

"No. But I'm beginning to think there's room for something more."

"Like what?"

He smiled, the dimple in his cheek flashing. "Someone who longs for adventure. Someone who's organized and dedicated and a bit of a control freak. Someone who filled a hole in my heart I didn't even know existed." He placed his hands on the side of her neck and cradled her head, his thumbs stroking her cheeks, sending ripples of warmth along her skin.

"Someone like you, Lena. I think I'm falling in love with you."

Fear erupted in her chest, scraping across her heart and soul with razor-sharp edges. She pushed away. "No, you can't be. It's too soon. We barely know each other." The tenderness she'd seen in his eyes died, replaced with dark disappointment. Her heart pounded in her chest. Her mind replayed another man who had professed love after only a few days. On this very pier. She turned her back, wrapping her arms around her waist, trying to sort out what had just happened.

She sensed Dix's agitation behind her, but she wasn't ready to face him. His quiet voice startled her when he spoke.

"Lena, I'm sorry. I should never have said anything. I never meant for this to happen. But it did. I should have kept my feelings to myself."

Her thoughts were a jumble of conflicting emotions. She was glad Dix cared for her, but the suddenness of his admission had yanked her back to the past and Peter. She didn't like comparing the two, but what else was she to think? People didn't fall in love overnight. What if he woke up tomorrow and realized it was all an infatuation? Peter's rejection had wounded her deeply. Being rejected by Dix would destroy her.

Lena inhaled a shaky breath and started back down the boardwalk toward her house.

"Lena?"

She shook her head. "I need to be alone right now. Please." She quickened her steps until she was jogging across the street and into her house, not stopping until she was safely on her bed with Oreo wrapped in her arms.

Then she cried.

Dix watched Lena until she disappeared into her house. Then he turned and ran his hands down the back of his neck in disgust and frustration. What a mess he'd made. And he had no idea how to fix it.

Being with Lena, holding her, had short-circuited his common sense, and he admitted his growing feelings for her. He hadn't intended to, but it had slipped out. Fear had blazed in her green eyes, and he'd realized in that instant he'd moved too quickly. He knew she was skittish about risking her heart. She'd told him what a whirlwind affair she'd had with Peter and how it had ended with her heart and her trust being crushed. And what did he do? Charge ahead like an idiot and practically restage the same plot. In the same location.

How could he have been so insensitive and so blind? His gut kicked when a new thought hit him. He had no indication that Lena felt the same way. She hadn't rebuffed his few advances, and he knew she enjoyed his company, but more than that was all wishful thinking on his part.

Dix closed his eyes, remembering the feel of her in his arms and her sweet orangey scent. She fit perfectly in his arms. She fit perfectly in his life. But he scared her off because he'd been too impatient. A stupid impulse he should have controlled.

He ran a hand through his hair and gripped the wooden railing, focusing his gaze on the water. In two weeks he'd be going home. Maybe if he worked round the clock he could cut that down by half. He didn't want to stay here any longer than necessary. It was best for both him and Lena if he went on his way.

Dix walked back across the street and into the Arnez house, grateful that Rick and his family were out tonight. He closed himself in his room and fired up his laptop. An appointment reminder popped up on the screen, and he realized he'd never gotten around to telling Lena he'd be out of town for a few days. He debated whether to call her or let Kelly explain it to her if she should ask.

No. That was the coward's way out. As soon as he had his emotions under control, he'd call her himself.

He'd created this mess. He could at least be man enough to face it.

Lena snuggled under the afghan and stared blindly at the old movie on TV as it came to an end. Why couldn't life be like a film? All the problems and questions tied up nice and neat, with everyone living happily ever after.

Her loose ends were in such a tangle she couldn't make sense of any of them. Dix was falling in love with her. No. He *thought* he was. What did that mean? What did she want it to mean?

She groaned and lifted Oreo into her lap. She wanted

it to mean the same thing it did to her. She thought she was falling in love with him, too. It should have been an easy thing to admit. He'd given her the perfect opening, but instead she'd bolted. Peter's legacy was still too etched on her psyche.

Lena touched her lips. He was such a tender, sweet man. And she wanted him in her life. But she needed more time to be sure.

The phone rang, and she willed herself to ignore it. But her heart wanted it to be Dix, and if it was, she didn't want to miss his call. She rose and hurried to the kitchen where she'd left it. It was Dix.

She held her breath and answered. "Hello."

"Hi. You weren't asleep, were you?"

The sound of his voice cheered her. "No. I'm watching an old movie."

"I wanted to let you know that I'm going to be away for the rest of the week. Tiffany and I are going down to Orlando to scout a few locations that I can't find here and meet with some people from the film commission."

Lena's heart sank. "Oh. When will you be back?"

"Sunday, probably."

The depth of her disappointment surprised her.

There was a long silence before he spoke again. "Will you miss me?"

She struggled for an appropriate answer. Saying yes might give him the wrong idea, but then so would saying no. She chose the cowardly middle ground. "I'll be pretty busy. We have our school carnival this weekend, and I'm on the planning committee, so…"

"So that's a no. You won't miss me at all?"

His teasing tone brought a flush to her cheeks. "Of course I will."

"Good. I'll miss you, too. We'll talk about—things when I get back."

"All right."

"Good-night, Sunshine."

"Good-night, Dix."

Lena hung up then placed her palms against her warm cheeks to cool them. A few days away from Dixon Edwards might be the best thing for both of them. But she missed him already.

## Chapter 9

The early morning air smelled fresh and clean, and the sun was warm and relaxing on her shoulders as she picked up the morning paper and started back down the driveway. It was a perfect day in St. Augustine. Mild temperatures, gentle breeze, clear sky. The kind of day you wanted to capture in a bottle and keep forever.

The kind of day she'd like to spend with Dix.

Lena slowed her pace as she neared her carport. Kelly's driveway was empty of vehicles. Of course she and Rick left early for work, but there should be another car parked there. Dix's rental car was missing.

He'd returned late Sunday night. She'd expected him to come over or to call, but she hadn't heard a word from him. This morning, she'd swallowed her pride and called Kelly to ask where he was.

He had scheduled another helicopter ride with an aerial photographer and wasn't due back until late afternoon.

Which meant she wouldn't see him until after school today. She'd missed him more than she'd expected the last few days. He'd called a couple of times, but only to say hello and fill her in on his progress. Nothing personal came up. She'd asked for space, and he was taking her at her word.

Now it was Monday, and she was beginning to wonder if she'd ever see him again. The sound of her ringtone sent her heart fluttering. Maybe it was Dix.

"Hi, sis."

Lena smiled when she recognized Jeanie's voice, hoping her disappointment wasn't evident in her tone. "Hello to you, too. What's going on?"

"Well, I have good news, bad news, and good news."

"Should I be sitting down for this?"

"No. Good news. I sold my house."

"That's great. And so fast."

"I know. Praise God for that. Good thing I had a small house and not one of those behemoths that are sitting on the market for years."

"And the bad news?"

"I'm officially out of work. We got the notice last Friday. Two more weeks, then it's all shut down."

"I'm sorry, Jeanie."

"Ah, but here's the other good news. I have another job already. And it's right there in St. Augustine."

"Wonderful. Are you coming home?"

"If you think you can stand us for a while."

"Of course."

"Well, this job is a godsend, but it's not permanent. It's only for the duration of the project. Mr. Sadler, the developer I'll be working for, wants to restore the old Sand Castle Motel down in south St. Augustine Beach. It should take six to nine months to complete, but that'll give me plenty of time to look for something more dependable."

"I'm so happy for you."

"He wants to meet with me this week, so I'll be driving over tomorrow evening and seeing him on Wednesday. Hope that's okay."

"Absolutely. I can't wait to see you."

Lena hung up the phone, her mood lightening considerably. Having Jeanie here would be fun, and it would distract her from thoughts of Dix and how she really felt about him.

So how did she feel? The question replayed incessantly in her mind all day at school.

She was no closer to an answer to that question when she pulled into the carport that afternoon, disappointed to see an empty driveway next door. Dix still wasn't home. Lena carried her work into the kitchen and stacked it on the table. The phone rang, and she held her breath, hoping it was Dix, but the ID revealed it was her baby sister calling.

Quickly she pushed the Talk button. Zanna only called if something was wrong. "Hi, kiddo. What's up?"

"Hi, sis. You have a few minutes to talk?"

Lena moved to the sofa and sat down. "Of course. I always have time for you."

"I'm glad you're home. I was afraid you would still be at school."

"No, but I am glad I came straight home today. What's wrong?"

Her sister released a long sigh. "Craig and I broke up."

"I'm sorry, Zanna. What happened?"

"Too much to explain on the phone. I'm thinking about coming home for a while."

"I'd love that. You know you're welcome any time. It's always nice to have a bestselling author in the house."

Zanna laughed. "Right. For a pointless little nothing of

a book. My editor is upset that I can't come up with another blockbuster idea. That whole *Hero* idea came out of
a sleep-deprived weekend working overtime. Who knew
it would be a hit?"

The line fell silent, and Lena waited for her sister to
continue.

"Lena, why isn't my life working out the way I wanted
it to?"

"I don't know, sweetie. I'm not sure any of us get the
life we plan on." Lena waited for a response, but the line
remained silent. "Suzanna?"

"I'm thinking about going back to church."

Lena closed her eyes and sent up a heartfelt prayer of
thanks. Her baby sister had turned away from God a long
time ago, and Lena had been gently urging her back to her
faith. Apparently God was doing the same thing. "That's
wonderful news. I hope you do."

"Do you think it'll help? I mean, will I feel better?"

"Yes. But don't look at church as some magic pill or
a social club that will make all your dreams come true.
Faith is about a relationship with God. About the condi-
tion of your heart."

"I know. I've got to do something, Lena. I can't go on
like this much longer."

"Why don't you come home? Jeanie and Molly are moving in here temporarily in a few weeks. We'd all be together again."

"That would be nice. A real family reunion. I'll think
about it. I have to go."

"I thought you wanted to talk."

"I know but… I have an appointment."

"Well, at least e-mail me off and on."

"I promise."

Lena couldn't shake off her sister's call. The tone of

Zanna's voice spoke of confusion and discouragement. Emotions that rarely surfaced in her bubbly and vivacious baby sister. She was the one who everyone believed would conquer the world. And she had. To a point. She'd written a charming and amusing book that had taken the country by storm. *Ten Hero Types Guaranteed to Make Your Dreams Come True.*

Suzanna was correct in calling it a pointless book. The so-called advice was hard to take seriously. Still, it had put her name on the map, opened doors, and given her financial security.

But her baby sister was capable of writing more than fluff. She was very creative and artistic. Whatever was going on with her, Lena rejoiced at Zanna's decision to go back to church. She only hoped her sister would embrace her faith again for the right reasons and not out of a desire for a quick fix.

Suzanna Butler was not known for her patience.

On Wednesday morning Lena cradled her cup of coffee in her hands, staring at the pool skimmer as it made its way around the aqua water. If only she could skim off the debris from her life as easily. Life had become very complicated since Dixon Edwards had arrived in town. Before spring break her future was clear, her goals clearly defined. She knew what she wanted and how she was going to get there. Everything was nice and neat. Organized.

Then Dix barged into her world and turned everything upside down. Her goals were in question, her dreams murky. And her emotions were in such turmoil she couldn't keep a coherent thought longer than a few minutes. But the scariest thing of all was that she had fallen in love with the man, and she didn't know what to do about it.

"Good morning, sister dear."

Lena looked up as Jeanie came and sat down on the other lounge chair with her own cup of coffee. "Did you sleep well?"

Jeanie nodded and took a sip from her mug. "I did, surprisingly. I never liked coming back to this house, but I guess time has lessened the old resentments. Now I find coming home, being with you, is so reassuring and comforting. You're the only family Molly and I have."

Lena's heart warmed. The Butler girls' childhood had been difficult, and she was pleased that Jeanie had come to terms with it.

"I forgot to tell you, Suzanna called yesterday."

Jeanie turned and looked at her, eyebrows raised. "Really? What brought that on? I haven't talked to her in six months or so."

"She's discouraged. Her editor isn't happy that she can't come up with a fresh idea for her next book."

Jeanie chortled deep in her throat. "Well, it's hard to top a book that leads women to believe there's a perfect man out there someplace. My Tim was as close as they come, but even I wouldn't call him perfect."

"Nonetheless, the book sold very well."

"I know, and it earned her scads of money and a brief moment of fame, but she's better than that. She should be writing something worthwhile, not that drivel."

"I agree, but that's her job, and it isn't going well at the moment."

Jeanie turned serious. "What's she going to do?"

"I don't know. She's very discouraged. I think that's why she wants to come home for a while, to relax and regroup."

"That might be fun. We haven't been together in a long time."

Lena nodded. "I'm glad I'm here for you girls to come home to. It's important to have a home."

Jeanie glanced over at her with a frown on her face. "What do you mean by that, exactly?"

"Just what I said. I'm glad you have a home to come back to when you need it."

"That has a very self-sacrificing tone to it."

"What do you mean?"

Her sister eyed her closely. "Are you still seeing Dix?"

"I'm not seeing anyone. Besides, he's been out of town on business."

"Is he back?"

"Yes. But I haven't seen him yet."

"How are things between you two?"

"We're friends."

"No. I'm not buying that for a moment. You're in love with the man."

Lena started to deny it, but Jeanie beat her to it. "Yes you are. I knew it from the first time I saw you two together. So what's the problem?"

"I've only known him a few weeks, for one thing."

"So? Have you told him how you feel?"

"Of course not."

"This is about Peter, isn't it?"

Lena inhaled sharply. How did her sister know about that?

Jeanie reached over and squeezed her forearm gently. "I ran into an old church friend of yours a few years ago. She mentioned it. I'm so sorry. Why didn't you tell us?"

"I didn't want to burden you—or admit how stupid I was. I was supposed to be the responsible one, remember?"

Jeanie stared at her, her eyes welling up with tears. "Oh Lena, I never realized…" She covered her mouth with her hands. "I'm so stupid. I should have seen it."

"What?"

"What we've done to you. We've turned you into our mother, and it's cost you a life of your own."

"No. No. Don't be silly; I'm grateful that I could be here for you girls."

"But what about you, Lena? Here I am moving back home like some irresponsible teenager, dragging my daughter along and messing up your future with Dix."

"You're not messing up anything. I love having you here."

"I know you do, but maybe you shouldn't. You should be building a life of your own, starting your own family with Dix. He adores you. And I suspect you've already fallen for him."

"I don't know."

"Look, Molly and I can move out. My new boss offered me a condo in one of his resorts free of charge while we work on this restoration project."

"No. I won't hear of it."

"Lena, you deserve a life of your own. You don't have to worry about us anymore. Suzanna and I are all grown up. If we run into trouble, we can solve it on our own. We shouldn't put you in the role of mom and run home to you whenever things get tough."

"You don't. Really."

"Promise me you'll think about what I said. Do what you want, Lena, what your heart tells you. We don't need you anymore."

"Thanks."

Jeanie rose and came over to give her a hug. "Silly. You know what I mean. Promise me you'll follow your heart this time?"

Lena smiled and patted her hand. "I'll try."

* * *

"I saw you pull in, and I couldn't wait to call and tell you my news. Guess what?"

Lena deposited her schoolwork on the table and chuckled aloud at her friend's excitement. With Kelly, getting a new potted plant was cause for celebration. "I haven't a clue."

"We're going to have another baby."

"Oh, that's great. At least, I'm assuming it's good news."

"Of course. We're thrilled. Maybe this time we'll get that little boy."

"I'm happy for you."

"We'll talk tomorrow. Have to you talked to Dix yet?"

"No, I haven't."

"Oh. That's strange. Well, I'm sure it's because he's so busy. We've barely seen him ourselves. I'll talk to you later."

The connection ended, and Lena smiled at her friend's good news. At least someone's life was going well. Another baby for the Arnez family. Kelly's second daughter had been an infant when they'd moved in next door, and Lena had often babysat.

She closed her eyes, remembering the moments, the sensation of holding the tiny little body. How would it feel to hold a child of her own? The thought shocked her. Never before had she considered a family of her own. Why now? A vision of Dix came into her mind. Her sisters had always told her that when she found the right man, she'd change her mind about having a family.

Maybe they were right. But how did she know if Dix was the right man or not? She wanted him to be. He had opened up new worlds to her in the short time she'd known him. Maybe this was another one.

A strange sadness formed in her chest. Dix had been

back for three days now and hadn't contacted her. Why? The answer was obvious. He'd decided to move on with his life. She couldn't blame him. He opens his heart to her, admits his growing feelings, and she runs away like a terrified rabbit.

Lena sat down at her computer, watching the screensaver slideshow of her adventures with Dix. She'd never felt this way before. So did that mean she was in love or merely bedazzled with his good looks and charm?

Placing her fingers on the keys, she opened a new document. Whenever she faced a difficult decision, organizing her thoughts and setting priorities usually gave her a clear road map to her solution. Maybe it would help her sort out her feelings for Dix.

She smiled as she began to list Dix's admirable qualities. He was the only one who'd appreciated her organizational skills. He'd freely admitted that she had improved his location scout. Most people hated her constant list making.

When her list of pluses far outpaced the minuses, Lena had to face the ugly truth. The only thing stopping her from loving Dixon Edwards was her own fear. He was exactly the kind of man she wanted. A strong, loving, Christian man. He made her feel brave and confident. When she was with him, she never worried about what was coming. He made her feel safe. He made her believe that she could have adventure and feel secure at the same time.

Lena stood and walked to the kitchen, staring at the phone. Was it too late for her and Dix? Had she ruined their relationship with her childish fears? There was only one way to find out. She picked up the phone and dialed.

Dixon Edwards stood on the vast beach at Anastasia State Park, marveling at how the ocean could make a man feel humble. He imagined it was a small glimpse of how he'd feel when he met his Savior face-to-face. The vastness of God. The smallness of man. And the immeasurable love that had bridged the gap between them.

He turned and started to walk. His thoughts quickly turned back to the other thing he felt on this endless, beautiful beach. Lonely. He missed Lena.

The chime of his cell phone intruded into his peaceful moment. His heart skipped a beat when he saw Lena's name on the screen. He braced himself and answered. "Hi."

"Dix, where are you?"

"I'm walking on the beach at the state park."

"I'd like to talk to you. Will you be back at Kelly's soon?"

He couldn't tell from her voice what she might want to talk about. "Why don't you come over here? I'll meet you near the observation walk."

"All right. I'll be there in a few minutes."

Dix's heart pounded in his chest. Had she missed him? Or did she want to talk about going their separate ways? He should have called her, but he'd been a coward. He didn't want to hear her say she didn't want to see him anymore.

Dix started across the sand, heading toward the meeting point. One way or the other it would be settled here today. If Lena didn't care for him, he'd go home tomorrow. Job or no job. Being in St. Augustine and not being with her would be too painful.

Lena hurried along the pedestrian walkover that crossed the dunes and connected to the beach. Her gaze scanned the white sands, looking for one familiar figure. Her heart skipped a beat when she saw him.

Dix.

He stood with his feet firmly planted on the sand, his

arms at his sides, his expression wary and expectant. Maybe she could bring back his smile and his dimple. If it wasn't too late.

She walked toward him, her uneven gait on the shifting sand echoing her shifting emotions. She stopped a few feet away from him, her courage fading. "Hi, Dix."

"Hello, Lena."

Her gaze soaked in the sight of him. Pale blue linen shirt hung over lightweight cargo pants, rolled up at the ankles. The breeze stirred his brown hair onto his forehead. His sky blue eyes were slightly narrowed, studying her closely, making her tense and edgy. Where did she start? How could she explain in a way he'd understand? "I'm glad you're back."

"Are you? I'm glad."

"Why didn't you call?" She cringed inwardly. Not how she wanted to start this conversation.

Dix grinned and relaxed. "I wanted to give you some space. I don't want to rush you, Lena."

Hope swelled in her heart. "Can we walk a little?"

Dix gestured for her to lead the way then fell in beside her. Lena searched for a good starting point, but nothing came to mind. Her hesitation opened the door for Dix.

"Lena, I need to apologize for what I said the last time we were together. I was only thinking about myself, and I ended up placing you in a difficult position. I never meant for that to happen. You'd shared your painful memories with me, and I turned around and made the same mistake. I scared you away, and I'm sorry. That's the last thing I ever wanted to do."

Lena stopped, forcing him to face her. "I know. But it's okay." She reached up and touched his cheek. "I'm glad you told me, because while you were gone I realized that I'm in love with you, too."

Dix's blue eyes bored in hers, searching for confirmation. "Are you sure? Lena, I'll give you all the time you need."

Lena shook her head. "I don't need any more time." She stepped closer and rested her hands on his chest. "My sister Jeanie told me it was time I followed my heart. I think she's right."

Dix gripped her shoulders, drawing her into his embrace. "I thought I'd lost you forever."

"I thought you'd moved on. You'd been home for days, and I hadn't heard from you."

"I'm a coward. I couldn't face your rejection."

"I was afraid. Of my feelings, of how quickly I'd come to care for you. And you were right. I had been letting my mistakes with Peter keep me from falling in love again."

Dix kissed her forehead. "No second thoughts?"

Lena slid her arms around his waist. "No. None. These last few days apart forced me to face a lot of things."

Taking her hand, Dix started to walk down the beach. "Such as?"

"What I really want for my future. I've been imagining myself alone for so long, I couldn't see it any other way."

"What about now? What do you see?"

"Us. Together. A home. Travel. A family of my own. A child of our own."

She sensed Dix tensing beside her.

He slowed his steps. "I thought you didn't want a family. That raising your sisters, having your students was enough for you."

"I thought so, too. Then I realized I was falling in love with you."

"What changed your mind?"

"Kelly got pregnant."

"What does that have to do with anything?"

"That's when I realized I loved you. I wanted to have a family. With you."

Dix had stopped walking beside her. She turned and smiled at him, but the expression on his face chilled her heart. Dix dragged a hand over his mouth and took several steps backward. Something was very, very wrong.

Dix turned his back, unable to look upon the fear and uncertainty in Lena's green eyes. He'd made an assumption about Lena, and because of his own weakness, his deep attraction to her, he'd allowed things to get out of hand. He dropped his hands and turned his back on her, searching frantically for the courage to tell her the truth. Praying for the right words to make her understand. Terrified of her response.

"Dix, what's wrong? Did I misunderstand you? I thought…"

"You didn't misunderstand anything, Lena. I'm in love with you. I think I have been from the first day."

"Then what is it?"

"I haven't been completely honest with you."

"About what?"

"Me. About my cancer." His courage faltered. *Please, Father, I need Your strength.* "Lena. I can't have children. At least, the odds are stacked against me."

Lena's eyes widened as she digested his announcement. "I don't understand. I thought you said you were cured."

"I am, but the treatments were aggressive, and there were consequences."

Lena stared at him, confused.

"I didn't tell you at first because it didn't seem to matter. You said you weren't interested in having a family. I'd been praying for the Lord to send a woman into my life who would be content without children. I thought you were the one."

Tears in Lena's eyes were like acid on his conscience. He'd never meant for this to happen. "Then I began to see you were meant to be a mother. You had so much love to give. I realized long before you told me that you didn't mean what you said, that you did want a family." He turned and faced her. "Lena, I can't give you that. Ever."

"Are you sure? I mean…"

"It's not impossible, but the odds aren't good."

"What else have you kept from me?"

"Nothing."

She shook her head. "You should have told me."

"I know. I guess I was hoping you meant what you said."

Lena scraped her fingers along the side of her head. "I need time to think."

Dix moved back another step. "Thinking won't change anything. Nothing will. This is a deal breaker. I know that." He started past her, but she reached out and grabbed his arm.

"Dix, I…"

He jerked out of her grasp. He couldn't face the pity in her eyes. "I've got work to do."

Lena's heart ached as she watched Dix stride angrily down the beach. He'd totally misunderstood her. He'd thrown her a bombshell then expected her not to react.

"Dix, wait. We need to talk about this."

He ignored her, jogging across the pedestrian bridge and out of sight. Lena sank down into the sand, hugging her knees, and let the tears come. Tears for him and the dreams that never could be.

When the tears subsided, she rose and started back up the beach. She had to find him and explain. It all made sense now. His comment about marriage and family not being the answer to everything, his dark moments, the sadness in his eyes. She'd told him she didn't want a family, and he'd taken her at her word, believing they had the same goals and dreams. She had to make him understand. It didn't matter to her. All that mattered was…

Lena stopped in her tracks. The realization of the depth of her feelings for Dix stole her breath. She loved Dix. Nothing else mattered. Her heart ached for him, for the life experience he'd lost. But it didn't matter to her. She loved him.

Her mind was clear as if she'd come out of a fog. Dix had shown her how to live again. To be less structured. Even convinced her to fly in a helicopter. To laugh. If the situation were reversed, how would she want him to respond?

Her confusion shifted quickly to righteous indignation. He hadn't even let her explain. How dare he drop a bombshell like that on her then run off? Now who was hiding?

She would not let him get away with this.

Lena pulled her car to a stop in the carport. Dix's car was here. She set her jaw and marched across to Kelly's back door. She walked in unannounced, stopping in the middle of the kitchen. Hands on hips. "Where is he?"

Kelly pointed over her shoulder. "In the guest room. What's wrong?"

Lena ignored her and marched to the door and pounded. "I want to talk to you. Now."

She waited, growing more angry by the moment. The gall of the man. "Dix! If you don't come out, I'll send Rick in to drag you out."

"He wouldn't do that," Dix called through the door.

"Yes I would."

Lena sent a grateful nod to her neighbor. The door

opened, and Dix faced her. Her anger nearly vanished at the sadness in his eyes. But they couldn't move forward until this was settled.

"Come out here. I can't talk to you in your bedroom."

"Lena, there's no point—"

"Oh." She reached over and grabbed his wrist, pulling him along behind her.

Rick grinned at them as they passed. "I told you she was a bulldog."

Lena didn't stop until they stood in the middle of her living room. She released his arm then turned to face him.

Dix planted his hands on his hips and stared. "What's this about, Lena?"

She rolled her eyes. "What do you think? You drop a bombshell on me, and then you don't even wait to see how I feel about it?"

"I saw how you felt."

"No. You saw my stunned surprise at learning about a painful event in your life. One that directly affects me, and you don't even give me time to digest it. You storm off, assuming I'm like Mona."

Dix rubbed his forehead. "No. I didn't think that. But Lena, you're right. This does affect you. I understand if you—"

"You don't understand anything." Lena released much of her anger but maintained her resolve. She had to make him see. "Dix, you blindsided me with your confession. Don't you think I deserve a little time to digest something that important?"

Dix glanced at the floor. "There's not much to digest. You want a family. End of story."

Lena shook her head. "No, it's not. You haven't let me tell you my part of the story."

"Lena…"

She moved forward and laid her hands against his chest. "It doesn't matter."

Doubt shaded his blue eyes. "You don't have to—"

"Please listen to me. It doesn't matter, because I love you. I want you. That's all that's important."

"It's not fair to you."

"Dix, I'm thirty-six years old. For all I know. I can't have children either. So what? There are other ways to build a family. We can adopt. We can be foster parents. Or hadn't you thought of that?"

"You'd be willing to do that?"

Her heart swelled with hope when she saw the shadow in his blue eyes lighten. "Of course I would. And what about miracles, Dix? We can always pray for one of those. Aren't you the one who always looks for possibilities?"

"Lena, what if you wake up one day and regret your choice?"

"Haven't you been pushing me to live my life, to embrace adventure? I only feel safe doing that with you. Think of the possibilities before us."

Dix wavered a moment then pulled her into his arms. "Lena, I love you. I have from the first moment I saw you." He chuckled softly against her ear. "You had me at *hello*."

She hugged him closer. "That's what I'd expect from a movie guy."

"Lena, you have to be sure."

"I am, but I think we still need to take time to get to know each other better."

"All the time you need." He pulled her closer. "I never thought I'd find a woman like you. Never even dreamed about it. I'll give you time, Lena. Space if you need it. I have a week before I have to leave. I won't push you, but I want to get to know you better, spend time together. Maybe you could come to Nashville for a visit when school's out.

You could stay with my sister, Denise. The one like you.
I think you two would hit it off."

"I'd like that. I didn't think I'd ever feel like this again.
I swore I'd never risk my heart again, but then you came
along and…"

"I was too cute to resist?"

She laughed. "Something like that."

## Chapter 10

Lena unlocked the back door, smiling when Oreo greeted her, wagging his tail and dancing in circles. "Are you excited, too, sweetie? Dix is coming for supper. We have a lot to do."

She disposed of her purse and schoolwork and quickly changed into a pair of yellow capris and a simple white top with a bird of paradise hand-painted on the front.

She and Dix had spent the last few days touring St. Augustine. This time as a couple in love and not searching out locations. Tonight was another new adventure. This was the first time she'd cooked for Dix, and she wanted everything to be perfect. She was a good cook, and Dix wasn't a picky eater. Still, she wanted to impress him. They had made no plans beyond agreeing to take their time getting to know one another, but she couldn't help thinking that someday she might be cooking for him on a daily basis. The thought made her smile.

Her fellow teachers had been bombarding her with questions about her good mood. All she'd told them was that she was seeing someone. Truth was, she felt like she was walking on air every moment now, counting the minutes until she saw him again.

Lena hummed a happy tune as she prepared the meal. Once the sauce was simmering and the oven heated, she took a moment to pass through the living room and tidy up. She straightened the mess on her computer desk then stepped outside to get the mail, sorting quickly through the small stack.

Bills. Bills. Flyer. Advertisement. The last envelope sent her heart into her throat. St. Johns County Board of Education.

Slowly she tore open the flap and pulled out the one-page letter. Joy erupted in her chest. She got the job. She'd been chosen as the new vice principal of First Coast Elementary School.

Her dream had come true. Finally, after a lifetime of uncertainty, of living a perpetual balancing act, she could take a deep breath and stop worrying what tomorrow would bring.

She picked up Oreo and hugged him, dancing around the room. "I got it. I got it." Now, no matter what happened, she'd be safe. Never again would she wonder if she could pay the bills. The ups and downs in the economy wouldn't affect her. Her retirement years were taken care of, and her health care would never be cut or withdrawn. She put Oreo down and exhaled a grateful breath. She'd never known such a feeling of relief. *Thank You, God.*

A new thought surfaced. Office. She'd have her own office. With a desk and a phone and file cabinets.

And lots of paperwork.

She wasn't looking forward to that part, but the trade-off would be worth it. "Okay, Oreo. The job isn't perfect, but what job is, huh?"

A twinge of sadness touched her heart. She'd miss her students. When school started next year, she wouldn't be there to greet the happy little faces. She wouldn't be there to ease their fears and show them the activity centers or teach them to read.

But she must make sacrifices to achieve her dreams. Now instead of having one class full of students, she'd have an entire building full. But less time to spend with them.

Lena closed her eyes and sighed. Finally, the pieces of her life were fitting together the way she'd planned. Walking back into the kitchen, she saw the sauce on the stove.

*Dix.*

Her heart sank. What would he say about her good fortune? And where did he fit in this new picture? The reality of it all came into focus, exposing the insurmountable obstacles between them. What had she thought their future held? To be together, one of them would have to give up a dream.

She'd never completely thought through her relationship with Dix. She'd been too bedazzled by her feelings, by his nearness, the fun she was having, and the new points of view he'd opened for her in the last few weeks.

She loved him. He was everything she'd ever dreamed of in a man. He made her feel safe. Protected. He made her feel as if she could do anything in the world as long as he was behind her, supporting her efforts. She woke up each morning anxious to be with him.

But now reality stared her in the face. She had to weigh her options. Security, her long-strived-for goal, her life's dream—or a life with Dix, on the move and uncertain. How did she choose between the man she loved and the job she'd worked so hard for?

Lena stuffed the letter back into the envelope and sat down at the kitchen table. What did she do now? For the first time since applying for the job, she wasn't sure she wanted it. Her heart sank to the pit of her stomach. Could she walk away from the security she needed to marry a man she'd only met a few weeks ago?

Lena turned her attention to the meal again, only to be interrupted by the ringing of the phone. She picked it up and barked a hello.

"Oh. What's wrong?"

Lena forced a calming breath into her lungs. "Hi, Jeanie. Nothing, why?"

"You sound strange."

"I'm preoccupied. I'm fixing dinner for Dix tonight."

"So why don't you sound happy? Something wrong between you two?"

"No. In fact, we've decided to pursue our relationship. Slowly. Take time to get to know each other better before we make any serious commitments."

"Sounds sensible and boring."

"Neither one of us wants to make a mistake."

"It's clear to anyone who cares to look that you two are crazy in love."

"That's what we want to make sure of."

"Uh-huh. So if it's not Dix, what's wrong?"

Lena fingered the letter lying on her table. "Nothing. I…" No point in denying it. Jeanie knew her too well. "I got the vice principal's position at school. The letter came today."

"That's great! Congrats. I know how much this means to you…. Wait. What about you and Dix?"

"I don't know."

"Lena, don't lose out on something special because you're afraid to risk your heart again."

"I'm not. But I have to think about you and Suzanna."

"What about us?"

"You and Molly will be moving home in a few weeks. You'll need me around. And things aren't going well for Suzanna. She might need to come home for a while, too. I really need to be here for you girls."

"No you don't. We can take care of ourselves."

"I know, but all we have is each other. I feel like I'm the only mother you really had, and a mom shouldn't stop being responsible for her kids."

The connection went silent. Lena thought the call had been dropped. "Jeanie?"

Her sister's voice was tearful when she responded. "Lena, I'm so sorry."

"About what?"

"I never realized until this moment what a huge burden we placed on you."

"You were never a burden."

"You spent most of your life standing in for our mother, always being the super-responsible one, the one Suzanna and I depended upon. You always put us first, repeatedly placing your own life on hold to make sure we had what we needed. In return we've taken you for granted. We expect you to be there to listen to our complaints, solve our problems, then we go back to our lives and forget all about you."

"That's not true."

"Really? Then why are you trying to be our anchor now? Why are you talking about being here for us? We're grown up. We don't need you, Lena. Not as a mom or a soft place to fall. We know you'll always be there for us, but you don't have to stay in St. Augustine to do that. Don't let your over-developed sense of responsibility or anything that's going on in my life or Zanna's come between you and Dix. If he asks you to run off tomorrow and get married, do it. Don't look back. Take him by the hand and run off to paradise. Please. You deserve that. You deserve him. He's a great guy. It only took me five minutes to realize that."

"He is. But I'm not going to make a rash decision."

"Sis, the only rash decision you could make would be to let him get away."

Dix leaned back in his chair and placed a hand on his stomach. "Miss Butler, your skills never cease to amaze me. That was the best shrimp creole I've ever had."

Lena smiled. "I'm glad you enjoyed it. It's my former neighbor's recipe. It was the first thing she taught me to make. I've tweaked it a little over the years."

Dix leaned forward, reaching over the table to touch the back of her hand. "Is this the kind of meal I can look forward to in the future? Because if so, I'm going to have to run a few extra miles each day or join a gym."

Lena tried to smile at his remark, but she was too distracted to concentrate on what he was saying.

He studied her a moment, the frown on his face deepening. "Lena, is everything all right? Something happen at school today?"

She couldn't keep her news from him forever. He had to know. Might as well be now. She rose and retrieved the envelope from the counter. She handed it to him and sat down, avoiding his gaze. A sick sense of dread pooled in her stomach while she waited for his response. When he finally looked over at her, she winced at the fear in his blue eyes.

"Congratulations. You've worked hard for this." He slipped the letter back into the envelope and shoved it toward her. "What are you going to do?"

"I'm not sure."

The muscle in Dix's jaw flexed. "What about us?"

"We can still see each other."

"Lena, I'm leaving soon. I can come and visit, but you know that's no way to conduct a relationship."

"You said you wanted to take time."

"Time, yes. Years, no."

"Maybe you could work out of St. Augustine for a while."

"My company is in Nashville. But a teacher can get a job anywhere."

"Not a vice principal job. This is what I've worked for all my life."

Dix clasped his hands in front of his chin. "I won't stand in the way of your dreams, Lena, but is this really the dream you want, or the one you're willing to settle for? A nice, safe life with no surprises? No adventure?"

"Dix." How could she make him understand? "I have to be sensible."

"Love isn't sensible."

"Love isn't a sure thing either."

Dix held up the letter. "This is a symbol of your fear and your misguided idea of security. It won't make you happy."

"It's not about being happy. It's about being responsible."

"At the cost of living without love?"

Dix stood and turned away, one hand on his hip, the other covering his mouth. When he turned back to face her, his eyes were moist.

"Don't do this, Lena. I know things between us happened fast, and I know it's crazy, but there it is. I love you, and I'm willing to give you all the time you need, but I'm not going to change my mind. I want to spend my life with you. I want to give you everything you've ever dreamed of."

Lena stood and moved away. The more he talked about

how much he loved her, the more nervous she became. Love was a promise no one could keep. The only one she could depend on was herself. People let you down. Her mom. Her dad. Peter.

She turned to face him and saw the pain and sadness flare in his blue eyes. Her heart shriveled inside her chest. "I don't want to hurt you, Dix, but it's not just the job. There are other things—"

"Such as?"

"My sisters, for one." Lena shook her head. She knew she was rationalizing but she couldn't help herself. Her logical side knew the girls didn't really need her in the same way as when they were growing up. It was her emotional side that was at war. She stood at a fork in the road, forced to choose between two dreams. In one direction was the security and safety she'd worked so hard for and longed for most of her life. In the other direction, her dream of love and adventure. Both choices came with risk and reward and a great deal of fear. So what exactly was she afraid of? Risking her heart again? Not being needed by her sisters?

"They're big girls, Lena. You're not their mother."

She ran her fingers through her hair. "I know, but…"

"But you don't love me enough to step out in faith."

"Yes, I do, but…" She turned and walked to the counter. It all made perfect sense in her head, but when she tried to explain it to him, it came out wrong. "I have to think of my future."

"I want to be your future, Lena." Dix's eyes turned dark as midnight, and his jaw clenched.

Lena took a step backward. She'd never seen him so angry, not even the night she'd accused him of soliciting money from Mrs. Watson. "Dix, try and understand."

He held up his hand, forestalling any explanation, his jaw working side to side. "What I understand is that you'd rather stay safe in your nice little predictable world than trust your heart to me and the wonderful future we can have together."

"It's not that. It's…" How could she make him understand her need for security and safety? She was so tired of living with a sense of calamity hanging over her head.

Dix placed his hands on his hips. "What is it, then? Help me understand what could have changed your mind so quick…." He dragged a hand across his mouth. "Oh. I get it. This is about me, isn't it?"

Lena shook her head. "No, it's me."

Dix turned and walked away, stopping at the back door. "I'm sorry, Lena, that I can't give you the future you want. But there's nothing I can do about it." He walked out.

It hit her then what Dix was talking about. "No. Dix, that's not it. Come back!" He thought she was pulling back because he couldn't have children. How could he believe that? She'd already told him it didn't matter to her.

Lena hurried out to the lanai, hoping to catch him, but Dix was already on Kelly's deck and going inside. Maybe it would be best to let him cool off before she spoke to him again.

Back in the kitchen she cleaned up, only partly aware of her actions. She placed the leftovers in the fridge, next to the chocolate cream pie she'd made. They'd never gotten around to sharing it.

A sob escaped her throat. Tears fell down her cheeks. She picked up the letter and went into the living room. This one piece of paper symbolized years of work and a lifetime of striving to achieve a sense of peace and security.

Dix had called it a symbol of her fear.

She opened the letter and read it again. She liked the prospect of a regular, predictable routine. A future where everything would be taken care of. She'd made the right decision.

So where was the feeling of relief and peace she'd assumed would accompany this moment? She'd known a moment of joy, of relief. Of accomplishment. But not peace. The only emotion she felt at the moment was heartache at the anguish in Dix's eyes.

She had a sick feeling that she'd made a mistake. One she could never undo.

Dix pulled his suitcase from the closet and tossed it on the bed. He didn't want to think about what had happened tonight. All he wanted to do was get as far away from Lena Butler as he could, because catching a glimpse of her, seeing her house, would tear his heart to shreds.

"Hey pal. Everything okay in here?"

Dix glanced over his shoulder at his friend. "Hey Rick. Yeah. I'm going to get a hotel room for the next couple of nights."

"Something come up?"

"Yeah. I've got several meetings in town, and it'll be easier to be close by." It was a lame excuse, and he knew Rick wasn't going to buy it. But he hoped he'd let it go and not push for another explanation.

"Okay. Anything I can do to help?"

"No. Thanks. I'll check in with you before I fly out on Saturday. Maybe we can meet for lunch before I go."

"Sounds good."

Dix waited for Rick to leave, but he remained in the doorway. He knew his friend was silently offering to listen if he wanted to talk, but at the moment all Dix wanted to do was run away. Childish response, but there it was.

"I'll help carry your stuff to the car when you're ready. Just give a shout-out."

Dix nodded, sinking onto the bed and resting his elbows on his knees. He wanted to pray, to seek guidance or answers or someone to blame, but he had no words. Only heartache.

Forcing himself to move, he packed the last bag then called out to Rick. Within five minutes he was loaded up and ready to leave. He promised Rick to talk to Kelly before he left town and managed to pull out of the driveway and onto Inlet Drive without once glancing at Lena's house. But when he steered onto the Bridge of Lions, his heart broke anew, and he found himself wishing he'd never come to St. Augustine.

Lena paced the living room, massaging her aching temples. She'd been over her decision a dozen times since Dix had walked out. She'd tried to think logically, with her head and not her heart, but her emotions were in turmoil, and trying to sort it all out was making her nauseous.

Glancing at the clock, she was surprised to see that Dix had left only an hour ago. It felt more like a decade. She had to take some action. She couldn't continue on this emotional merry-go-round. She had to talk to him again. At the very least make him understand her choice had nothing to do with the side effects of his cancer. It had to do with stability for her future.

A niggling finger of doubt skittered into her conscience. No. She'd made the right decision. She had. Accepting this position was the logical, responsible thing to do.

The doubt refused to be eased.

Crossing her arms over her chest, she walked into the kitchen and stared down at the letter that had changed everything. She'd been so sure when she received the notification, but she hadn't been prepared for the pain she'd seen in Dix's eyes or the deep aching loss in her own heart.

She couldn't sleep unless she tried to fix this mess.

Gathering her courage, she walked across the drive and knocked on Kelly's door. The kitchen light came on, and the back door opened. "Hey. Can I come in?"

Kelly stepped aside to let her enter. "What's going on?"

"Dix and I had a…disagreement. I need to talk to him and explain. He misunderstood some things I said."

"I'm sorry, Lena, but he's gone."

"Gone? Where?"

Kelly crossed her arms over her chest. "He came in, packed up, and moved into town."

Lena's heart twisted into a cold knot. "Why?"

"He said he had a lot of work to finish before he went home, and it would be easier to stay in town."

Lena sank onto a chair. "Is he coming back?"

"No. Look, Lena, I don't know what happened between you two, but I'm not happy about it. And I don't want to be caught in the middle. You're both my friends. You want to tell me what happened?"

"I got the promotion." She scraped her hair off her forehead. "I'll be the vice principal next year."

Kelly sighed. "And you decided it was safer to take the job than marry Dix?"

Lena stared at her friend. "I thought you'd understand, of all people."

"I do. But that doesn't mean I agree with you. I think you've thrown away something special. Something that only comes around once in a lifetime if we're lucky. I think you've let a man who adores you, who is perfect for you, get away because you're afraid."

"I'm not afraid. I'm trying to be realistic."

"And if I know you, unwilling to compromise."

"Why am I the one who always has to compromise?"

Kelly reached over and squeezed her forearm. "Everyone gives up something for love, Lena. Life is a series of compromises. People who live life completely on their own terms usually end up alone and miserable. Is that what you want, Lena?"

"No, but…"

"Then you've got to let go of your fear and step out in faith. Or you'll regret it the rest of your life."

Lena rolled over and glanced at the clock beside her bed: 5:00 a.m. She might as well get up. She'd seen every hour on the clock since going to bed. Her thoughts had churned like a category-four hurricane all night.

Rising, she padded to the bathroom in search of aspirin. Her head throbbed, and every muscle in her body ached. If she didn't know better she'd think she was coming down with the flu, but the truth was she was heartbroken. Taking the job was the right thing to do. So why did it feel so awful?

She brushed her hair and put on her morning lounge pants and shirt then walked slowly into the living room. Her gaze settled on the little battery-operated fan on a string that Dix had given her. It brought all his best qualities to her mind. His smile. His sense of humor. His passion for life.

She wanted to cry, but the tears refused to come. She'd used them up last night. Forcing herself to follow her prescribed morning routine, she fixed the coffee, sliced some fruit, and prepared her cereal. It all tasted like sand in her mouth.

She shoved the food away. Might as well get ready for work. Maybe being busy would help her sort through her dilemma. But the hot shower had no effect on her mental or physical state. Her head still throbbed, and her heart felt as if it were squeezed in a vise. There was no way she could work today. She'd have to call in sick.

Lena had barely hung up the phone with the school when it rang again. The caller ID showed Jeanie's name. For a moment she considered ignoring the call. But part of her needed the comfort of her sister. Besides, something might be wrong. Her sister never called this early. "Hi, Jeanie. Is everything all right?"

"I thought you might need to talk."

"About what?"

"Kelly called me. She was worried about you. So am I. What happened between you and Dix?"

Lena sank down onto the sofa. "It wasn't meant to be, that's all."

"Lena, that's ridiculous. Why are you letting this job come between you two?"

"I'm not. This is something I've worked hard for."

"I know, but is it what you really want?"

Was it? She'd always thought so.

"I don't think it's what you want at all. I think you're afraid. You've got your fists so tightly wrapped around your fear of being hurt again and your need for control, you can't even see it's become a prison."

"That's not true. I just want to be prepared in case something happens."

"When have you ever had control over your life?"

"Never. That's what I'm afraid of."

"And have all your plans and lists and organization prevented anything bad from happening?"

"No."

"Were you able to control Mom's drinking or Dad's absence?"

"No."

"And were you able to control Peter and his criminal ways?"

"No, but—"

"No one has control in this world, Lena. Control is an illusion."

"This isn't about control. It's about security and planning for the future."

Jeanie was silent a moment. "Tim and I planned for the future. We had everything worked out. But we couldn't foresee him dying so young. No more than you can predict how your life will unfold. What if Dix died tomorrow? Would you regret letting him walk away? Missing out on time with him, no matter how short?"

Lena rested her head on the back of the sofa. She had only one answer for that. "Yes."

"That's what it comes down to, Lena. Your future happiness or your future loneliness. Which is it going to be?"

A light rain had started, and Lena took her glass of tea and moved out to the lanai. Listening to the rain had always soothed her. Curling up on the lounge chair, she invited Oreo to join her then settled back, closing her eyes and letting the rain and the sweetly scented Florida breeze seep into her being. The moment was brief. Thoughts of Dix, bits of advice and admonishment from her sister and her friend quickly intruded.

Everyone seemed to have an answer. Everyone but her. Oreo moved from her side to her lap and she smiled, stroking his long hair. He always knew when she was upset. He was the only one who knew her. The only one who cared— No. God cared. And He was the only one she'd not bothered to seek advice from.

Quickly she rose and retrieved her Bible and study books. As an afterthought she pulled her old Bible from the bookcase and carried them all out to the patio table. There were certain passages in her old, worn edition that still comforted her.

Lena spread out the literature on the table, starting with the fruit of the Spirit study book. As she read over the nine fruits, her mind focused on the word *peace*. It was something she craved. Peace equaled freedom from fear. From uncertainty. From the scary surprises of tomorrow. A note in her guide pointed out that the fruit of the Spirit was a by-product of living for God.

So why didn't she have peace in her heart? What was she missing?

Opening her old Bible, she flipped through the pages. A slip of notepaper slid out onto the table. She picked it up, recognizing it as a prayer list she'd made as a teenager.

*Dear God,*
*1. Please help me take care of my sisters.*
*2. Please keep us from being homeless.*
*3. Please send me a friend to help.*

Tears welled up in her eyes, and her chest compressed with remembered fear. Some days she'd felt so alone, so overwhelmed by the responsibility of caring for her sisters. But now, looking at this list, she could see clearly that God had answered each and every prayer.

He'd given her the strength and wisdom to manage the house and her siblings. He'd kept a roof over their heads, even when she was certain they would be evicted. And He'd sent her Mrs. Russell, the kindly neighbor who had been her mentor, her comfort, and her surrogate grandparent.

How had she not seen this before? How could she have believed for one second it was all her own determination that had kept her family together? She wiped the tears from her eyes.

Dix had tried to tell her God had been always at her side, but she hadn't seen it. She realized Dix had been right about something else, too. She had been angry at God. She'd blamed Him for not healing her mother, for not changing her father, for making her life so hard. Mostly she blamed Him for sending Peter into her life.

A jolt of realization sent shame rushing through her veins. She'd been so desperate to leave her life of responsibility and obligation, she'd grasped the first escape she found—Peter. And she'd expected him to be her savior and make her world right and fair.

Lena ran her palm across the worn and faded page of her old Bible. Her habit of slipping prayer lists between the pages had started at age twelve. Idly she flipped over a few more pages, not surprised to find another note, dated before she went off to college in Tampa. The words of this prayer stole her breath.

*Please, God, send me a man to love me. Someone who will make me laugh. Someone who will take me on adventures and make me feel safe.*

She blinked the tears from her eyes. He had. He'd sent Dix.

And she'd sent him away.

A sudden restlessness came over her, and she stood and walked out of the lanai, not stopping until she reached the covered pavilion at the end of the pier. She used to come out here frequently to be alone, to read a book or study her Bible in her rare free moments. It felt good to be back. Lifting her face to the heavens, she opened her hands, palms up, releasing all the fear and the control to the One who was truly in charge.

*Forgive me, Father. I've been looking for peace in my own abilities and not in the source of peace itself. You. I'm tired of living my life bound by fear and a need for control. I'm giving it all to You.*

She stood motionless, releasing each worry, each concern, each doubt into His care. Slowly her mind was filled with a sweet, penetrating peace. She opened her eyes and smiled. A sense of security like she'd never known filled her being. The Lord had guided her safely through every obstacle before, and He would guide her through whatever obstacles—no, possibilities—she and Dix would face.

Together.

She knew what she had to do now. *Please, Lord. Father. Don't let me be too late.*

## Chapter 11

Lena walked into Kelly's kitchen, calling her name. She had to find Dix. She had to tell him she'd been a frightened, faithless fool in sending him away.

Kelly hurried toward her, her expression reflecting her concern. "What's wrong?"

"I have to find Dix. Please, tell me where he is."

Rick joined his wife. "I'm sorry, Lena, but he's leaving today. He's probably on his way to Jacksonville already."

"No." Lena grabbed Kelly's arm. "I have to talk to him. I have to tell him I love him, that nothing else matters."

Kelly smiled and squeezed her hand. "Praise God. I didn't think you'd ever come to your senses. What happened?"

"I'll tell you later. I can't let Dix leave without letting him know. What am I going to do?"

Rick fumbled with his cell phone. "Okay, I just texted him. He's in line to go through security check. His plane doesn't leave for another hour and a half. It'll take you forty minutes or so to get to Jacksonville. You've got time if you leave now."

"Did you tell him I was coming?"

"No. Do you want me to?"

Her mind ran through her options. "No. I have to do this in person."

The drive to the airport was interminable. She parked the car then pulled out the small suitcase she'd brought with her. She stopped outside of the security checkpoint to concourse B and scanned the crowd. When a friendly looking couple came near, she asked them to take her picture with her phone. She positioned her suitcase at her feet, adjusted the trinket around her neck, then flashed a big smile.

After thanking the couple, she moved off to the side and sent the picture. She sent up a prayer as well. *Please, Father, don't let it be too late.*

All she could do now was wait.

Dixon Edwards slumped in his seat in the boarding gate area, worrying his bottom lip with his thumb. He should never have allowed himself to cross the line with Lena. He'd guarded his heart for a long time, knowing exactly what his future held. It didn't include a wife and family.

But she'd slipped into his heart without warning, and instead of locking down his emotions, he'd allowed his infatuation to blind him to the consequences. As a result, he'd placed her in the position of having to choose between her dream job and her feelings for him. It was cruel and unfair. She'd made it clear from the start what her goal in life was. He'd distracted her, imposing his own dreams onto her. He'd have to apologize and ask her forgiveness.

But not until he quit hurting. The mere thought of her

brought a million blades of pain through his heart. It might be a long time before he could withstand the sound of her voice. Dix closed his eyes, seeking clarity from above. He was too confused and hurting to think things through without help. He inhaled a deep breath and started at the beginning.

He'd been a contented and satisfied man when he'd arrived in St. Augustine—at peace with his situation and his future. Until he'd met gentle Lena Clare, a woman he wanted to spend his life with. His first mistake.

Falling in love with her had uncovered a few faith flaws he needed to address. The most disturbing was a latent resentment toward the Father for closing the door on his future as a family man. The other, his own failure to fully trust that the Lord knew best.

Dix shifted in his seat, remembering what Rick had said about believing that the Father had given him all the blessings he deserved and there were no more. He didn't believe that either. God didn't limit His love or His blessings. So where did that leave him?

In love with a woman he couldn't have. And having to live with the pain the rest of his life.

His cell phone vibrated against his heart. He pulled it out of his shirt pocket and frowned. Someone was sending him a picture. He tapped the screen, inhaling sharply at an image of Lena. It took him a moment to decipher what he was seeing. She was standing in front of an airport security entrance, a suitcase on the floor in front of her. Her hand was touching something around her neck that looked like a little…fan. The one he'd given her. His heart raced. The time stamp read thirty seconds ago. Which meant—

Bolting from his seat, Dix grabbed his gear and headed toward the main airport. Lena was here.

* * *

Lena paced in small circles, her gaze darting toward the walkway leading from the gates. Her heart pounded so violently in her chest it was hard to breathe. What if he didn't understand her picture? What if it didn't matter? What if he was so hurt and angry he couldn't forgive her? What if…

"Lena!"

She turned, her heart flying out of her chest and tears welling up in her eyes. Dix was hurrying toward her, his blue eyes filled with love.

He stopped in front of her, searching her face. "What are you doing here?"

"I don't want to be alone and safe anymore. I want adventure. With you."

Dix dropped his gear and wrapped his arms around her, lifting her off the ground. "Lena, I thought I'd lost you forever. I'm sorry I pushed you. I want you to be happy, even if it means staying here. I'll find a way to make it work…"

Lena touched his lips. "I'm not taking the job, Dix. You were right. I was a prisoner of fear. I've let it all go. I've given it to the Lord once and for all."

"Are you sure? You have to be sure, because there are things I can't change. Like a family…"

She smiled and kissed him. "If the only family we have is you, me, and my dog, that's enough. But I think there's room in our hearts for children who might need a lot of love and adventure, too."

Dix pulled her into his arms, kissing her lips with a tenderness that made her heart ache.

The announcement of his flight number intruded rudely on their reunion. Dix released her, keeping his hands on her arms. "I have to go. But I'll be back next week. We'll make plans for the future."

"June."

"What?" He searched her face.

"This June would be a perfect time for a wedding, don't you think? As soon as school is out."

"I love you, Lena. I'll spend the rest of my life proving it to you." He touched her cheek. "I've got to go. I'll call you when I get to Nashville."

She nodded and blew him a kiss. He went through security then disappeared down the corridor.

For the first time in her life, Lena felt peace. Peace with her Lord. Peace with herself. And peace with the future ahead.

# *Epilogue*

Lena checked the clock on her computer, comparing the time to the wall clock in the kitchen. Dix's flight was due in an hour ago. He should be here by now. She'd called his cell, but it kept going to voice mail. What could have happened?

Five more minutes passed, and her concern grew. She moved toward the back door to run over to Kelly's and see if she'd heard anything. Her cell phone rang, and she pulled it from her pocket. Dix. Finally. "Where are you? Are you all right?"

Dix's laughter met her ears. "Hello to you, too, Sunshine."

She closed her eyes, imagining his dimple flashing. "I was getting worried."

"I'm fine. Why don't you come and see for yourself?"

"Where are you?"

"Look out your front window."

She moved to the front window, pulled the drapes aside, and searched the front yard and the driveway. Then her gaze drifted to the pier across the street. Dix was waving at her.

Giddy joy bubbled up in her chest. She tossed the phone into the chair and hurried out the door, not stopping until she reached his arms. Dix swung her around then set her down, pulling her into a kiss. "I never knew a week could be so long," he whispered against her cheek.

Lena hugged him tighter, anticipating the not-too-distant moment when they'd be able to hold each other for the rest of their lives. "I missed you."

"Good. I want you to miss me." He released her and stepped back, his dimple flashing. "I have something for you."

"Presents?" Having Dix back beside her was present enough.

"Sort of." He pulled out a small velvet box and opened it.

The sparkling diamond inside took her breath away. "Oh Dix."

Wariness shone in his blue eyes. "If it's not what you want, we'll exchange it, but I wanted you to have something to wear this weekend to show everyone."

Dix knew her so well. They'd never discussed rings, but its setting was exactly what she would have chosen. "I love it."

He slipped the sparkling stone onto her finger. It was a perfect fit. Dix took her hand and kissed her palm then pulled her close again. "Are you ready to start our adventure together?"

"Oh yes."

"Good, because I have one more thing to give you to seal the deal." He handed her a blue envelope. "In case you get cold feet. There's still six weeks until the wedding. I don't want you to start second-guessing yourself and change your mind."

"Not a chance." She undid the flap and pulled out two airline tickets. She glanced up at him. His dimple flashed. Opening up the small folder, she gasped as she read the destination. "Beijing. We're going to Beijing?"

"Seems like the perfect place for a honeymoon, and I hear there are plenty of good photo ops on the Great Wall."

Lena giggled. "And you thought a trip to China would guarantee me showing up at the church?"

"Couldn't hurt."

She reached up and stroked his cheek. "Nothing could keep me away. I want to be your wife, Dix."

"Oh my beautiful dreamer. I want to make all your dreams come true." Dix pulled her into his arms and kissed her with all the love and promise in his heart.

\* \* \* \* \*

# REQUEST YOUR FREE BOOKS!

## 2 FREE CHRISTIAN NOVELS
## PLUS 2
## FREE
## MYSTERY GIFTS

H E A R T S O N G

P R E S E N T S

---

**YES!** Please send me 2 Free Heartsong Presents novels and my 2 FREE mystery gifts (gifts are worth about $10). After receiving them, if I don't wish to receive any more books I can return the shipping statement marked "cancel." If I don't cancel, I will receive 4 brand-new novels every month and be billed just $4.24 per book. That's a savings of 20% off the cover price. It's quite a bargain! Shipping and handling is just 50¢ per book in the U.S.* I understand that accepting the 2 free books and gifts places me under no obligation to buy anything. I can always return a shipment and cancel at any time. Even if I never buy another book, the two free books and gifts are mine to keep forever.

159 HDN FT97

Name                                (PLEASE PRINT)

Address                                                              Apt. #

City                         State                         Zip

Signature (if under 18, a parent or guardian must sign)

### Mail to the **Reader Service:**
### IN U.S.A.: P.O. Box 1867, Buffalo, NY 14240-1867

Not valid for current subscribers to Heartsong Presents books.

\* Terms and prices subject to change without notice. Prices do not include applicable taxes. Sales tax applicable in N.Y. This offer is limited to one order per household. All orders subject to credit approval. Credit or debit balances in a customer's account(s) may be offset by any other outstanding balance owed by or to the customer. Please allow 4 to 6 weeks for delivery. Offer available while quantities last. Offer valid only in the U.S.

**Your Privacy**—The Reader Service is committed to protecting your privacy. Our Privacy Policy is available online at www.ReaderService.com or upon request from the Reader Service.

We make a portion of our mailing list available to reputable third parties that offer products we believe may interest you. If you prefer that we not exchange your name with third parties, or if you wish to clarify or modify your communication preferences, please visit us at www.ReaderService.com/consumerschoice or write to us at Reader Service Preference Service, P.O. Box 9062, Buffalo, NY 14269. Include your complete name and address.

# REQUEST YOUR FREE BOOKS!

## 2 FREE INSPIRATIONAL NOVELS
## PLUS 2
# FREE
## MYSTERY GIFTS

*Love Inspired*

---

**YES!** Please send me 2 FREE Love Inspired® novels and my 2 FREE mystery gifts (gifts are worth about $10). After receiving them, if I don't wish to receive any more books, I can return the shipping statement marked "cancel." If I don't cancel, I will receive 6 brand-new novels every month and be billed just $4.49 per book in the U.S. or $4.99 per book in Canada. That's a savings of at least 22% off the cover price. It's quite a bargain! Shipping and handling is just 50¢ per book in the U.S. and 75¢ per book in Canada.* I understand that accepting the 2 free books and gifts places me under no obligation to buy anything. I can always return a shipment and cancel at any time. Even if I never buy another book, the two free books and gifts are mine to keep forever.

105/305 IDN FVW5

| Name | (PLEASE PRINT) | |
|------|------|------|

| Address | | Apt. # |
|------|------|------|

| City | State/Prov. | Zip/Postal Code |
|------|------|------|

Signature (if under 18, a parent or guardian must sign)

Mail to the **Reader Service:**
**IN U.S.A.:** P.O. Box 1867, Buffalo, NY 14240-1867
**IN CANADA:** P.O. Box 609, Fort Erie, Ontario L2A 5X3

**Are you a subscriber to Love Inspired books
and want to receive the larger-print edition?
Call 1-800-873-8635 or visit www.ReaderService.com.**

* Terms and prices subject to change without notice. Prices do not include applicable taxes. Sales tax applicable in N.Y. Canadian residents will be charged applicable taxes. Offer not valid in Quebec. This offer is limited to one order per household. Not valid for current subscribers to Love Inspired books. All orders subject to credit approval. Credit or debit balances in a customer's account(s) may be offset by any other outstanding balance owed by or to the customer. Please allow 4 to 6 weeks for delivery. Offer available while quantities last.

---

**Your Privacy**—The Reader Service is committed to protecting your privacy. Our Privacy Policy is available online at www.ReaderService.com or upon request from the Reader Service.

We make a portion of our mailing list available to reputable third parties that offer products we believe may interest you. If you prefer that we not exchange your name with third parties, or if you wish to clarify or modify your communication preferences, please visit us at www.ReaderService.com/consumerschoice or write to us at Reader Service Preference Service, P.O. Box 9062, Buffalo, NY 14269. Include your complete name and address.

LIDIR12

# *Reader Service*.com

## Manage your account online!

- Review your order history
- Manage your payments
- Update your address

---

*We've designed
the Reader Service website
just for you.*

---

## Enjoy all the features!

- Reader excerpts from any series
- Respond to mailings and
  special monthly offers
- Discover new series available to you
- Browse the Bonus Bucks catalogue
- Share your feedback

*Visit us at:*
## ReaderService.com

RS12